DREAM DEM(

Diana could have sworn that the floor had tilted,
like the deck of a ship. She stared down at the vinyl
tiles. Was it her imagination, or was the marbled
pattern rippling like shallow waves on a beach?
Impossible.

But the room *was* shaking. She turned round,
alarmed. The cups were dancing on their hooks.
Crockery chinked as it vibrated. Was it an
earthquake? No, that was ridiculous.

She braced herself against the back of the chair.
The vibrations were getting stronger. A cup,
half-filled with cold coffee, did a kamikaze leap off
the table and shattered, sending brown liquid
coursing across the floor. A china pig did a jig
before throwing itself, lemming-like, from the shelf
above the sink. Diana pulled herself to her feet and
tottered towards the door, clinging to the edge of
the table for support. It felt as though the whole
room were on roller-skates.

There was a sound like a sheet being torn in half
and a huge black crack snaked across the wall
above her. Then there was a seething, whispering
hiss. The crack bulged. Something was trying to
climb through it. Diana saw the tips of fingers
pushing their way through the disintegrating
plaster. Long, dirty fingernails scraped at the
wall . . .

About the Author

Anne Billson was born in Southport in 1954. She studied graphic design at the Central School of Art and Design, and worked as (among other things) a secretary, a cinema cashier and a photographer before a freelance writer and film critic. Her interests include opera, gardening and skin diseases.

Anne Billson lives in London.

Dream Demon

Anne Billson

NEW ENGLISH LIBRARY
Hodder and Stoughton

First published in Great Britain
in 1989 by New English Library
paperbacks

An NEL Paperback Original

British Library C.I.P.

Billson, Anne, *1954–*
    Dream demon.
    I. Title
823'.914[F]

ISBN 0-450-48636-2

Printed and bound in Great Britain
for Hodder and Stoughton
Paperbacks, a division of Hodder
and Stoughton Limited, Mill
Road, Dunton Green, Sevenoaks,
Kent TN13 2YA (Editorial Office:
47 Bedford Square, London
WC1B 3DP) by Richard Clay
Limited, Bungay, Suffolk.
Photoset by Rowland
Phototypesetting Limited, Bury St
Edmunds, Suffolk.

MONDAY

Diana's grandfather tried to warn her. He was dead, so it wasn't easy for him. But he did what he could.

She was wandering around in the ruined city when he forced his way through to her. She was surprised to see him there, partly because he'd been dead for so long and partly because it was the first time she'd seen anyone else in the city, even though she dreamt about it quite regularly. Anyway, here he was. She stood on tiptoe and kissed him on the cheek.

He told her to be very, very careful.

Diana assured him that she would look after herself. 'And even if I don't,' she added, 'Oliver certainly will. You don't know Oliver, do you? But I'm sure you'd like him.'

'Ah, yes,' her grandfather said. 'Oliver. That reminds me . . .'

But then Diana woke up.

For a while, she couldn't remember where she was. It was all so dreamlike that she wasn't so sure that she *had* woken up. Low shafts of sunlight pierced the room at odd angles. Specks of dust were dancing in the air. There was music in the background: a faint soprano scaling the heights of opera's greatest hits.

Diana was sitting, half-lying, on a couch. There were women bent over her. They were talking in hushed tones, as though she were an invalid.

I

She wasn't an invalid, of course. She was quite well.

She looked down at her hands. She had elegant hands. The manicurist told her so. Everyone told her so. She'd stopped biting her nails when she was fifteen.

It was the sapphire on her ring finger that jogged her into remembering where she was. How could she have forgotten? She was in the fitting room at Kureishi and Co, just off Bond Street. The wedding was only two weeks away. There was still such a lot to do, and she was sitting here, doing nothing, while a lot of pernickety women fussed about a dress which she would be wearing only once in her life.

She caught sight of her reflection in one of the mirrors on the opposite wall. She looked pale, despite all the sunbed sessions at the club. Her face floated small and fragile above a sea of white satin and lace.

Three women, their lips pursed around spare pins, were tinkering with the hem and bodice. Diana thought of the women as Gorgons. Two of them were middle-aged-going-on-elderly and completely lacked a sense of humour. Their sour expressions could have turned anyone to stone. Diana had the feeling they disapproved of her, though she couldn't imagine why. They probably disapproved of everyone, except Rachel. The third seamstress was younger, prettier than the other two. They gave her a hard time.

'Dozed off, did you?' asked Rachel. She looked up from the paper patterns spread over her desk. Diana nodded.

Rachel stood up. She picked her way carefully around the bunched satin and perched on the couch next to her client. Diana's heart sank. This was all part of the personal service, she supposed, but she could have done without it. Rachel was pushy. She was forever trying to persuade Diana to go with her on some sort of weekend course which forced its participants through various humiliating mental hoops. The idea, as far as Diana

2

could make out, was for them to harness their untapped potential and achieve their life-objectives, whatever those might be. Diana thought it sounded awful. She imagined the course churning out hundreds of people like Rachel: all of them briskly self-confident and supremely insensitive.

'I was having a peculiar dream,' she said, hoping to keep the conversation away from Rachel's pet topics. It had been peculiar, though. She'd been talking to her grandfather, which was strange. She hadn't dreamt about him for years.

'Do *you* have dreams?' she asked Rachel.

'Sometimes,' Rachel replied. 'But I don't always remember them. Sometimes I dream about my dresses falling to pieces in public and showing my clients' underwear. Then I get sued. They're real nightmares, I can tell you.'

'I always remember my dreams,' Diana said. 'Sometimes, I dream about a ruined city. There's no one there. Nothing ever happens.'

'Really?' said Rachel. 'How interesting.' Her head suddenly dipped forward. She swooped on Diana's sleeve. 'How many times have I told you?' she snapped at the youngest of the seamstresses. 'You must *always* remove the pins.'

The two older women looked smug. Diana felt sorry for the girl, who was blushing furiously.

Rachel rolled her eyes in exasperation. Then she said something very odd to Diana. She said: 'Your grandfather is a stupid old man. Take no notice of him.'

Diana blinked and said: 'I beg your pardon?'

'The ring,' Rachel said. 'I was admiring your engagement ring again.'

'I thought you said something about my grandfather.'

'Why on earth should I do that?' Rachel asked, tilting her head to one side. 'No, I was wondering how much it cost.' She seized Diana's left hand and eyed the sapphire greedily.

Everyone eyed it. It was difficult not to. Diana would have preferred something a little less ostentatious. A plain solitaire, perhaps. But Oliver had been quite adamant.

'You can't be selfish about these things,' he'd said. And there she was, thinking she was being rather *unselfish*. 'No one wants to see you wearing a discreet little diamond. You've got to give them something to talk about. You've got to give them a *rock*.'

And, after all, it was his money. Diana had given in. She was getting used to the sapphire, though she suspected that her mother still considered it just the tiniest bit vulgar.

Rachel, on the other hand, wouldn't have known vulgarity if it had smacked her in the eye. Diana had fought to keep the dress fairly simple. No, she didn't want embroidery or smocking. Nor did she want puff sleeves. She didn't want to end up looking like a milkmaid.

Rachel had had enough of the ring for now. She dropped Diana's hand and smiled her practised smile. 'You're going to look absolutely gorgeous,' she said.

Her tone was patronising, but Diana managed to gasp out a thank you, trying not to breathe as one of the seamstresses nipped in the fabric around her waist.

Everyone thought her naïve, she knew. They thought they could be nice to her face, and then say bitchy things behind her back. Rachel was no exception. She sometimes called Diana a 'Sloane' when she thought she was out of earshot. Diana had once overheard herself described as someone who had 'never done a day's work in her life'. Rachel frequently made snide references to Diana's 'private income'. Diana felt stung on such occasions. It wasn't fair. Her allowance wasn't *that* big. And she *had* worked: for nearly two years at a nursery school. She could easily have got a job in publishing, or perhaps in

4

one of the salesrooms, like some of her friends. But she didn't see the point. There were other people who needed the work more than she did.

She didn't care for Rachel at all, and she was sure the feeling was mutual. They had never been friends at school. It was only at the insistence of her mother that Kureishi and Co had been approached about the dress. Rachel was still peeved at having been overlooked for the royal wedding commissions. Diana was minor compensation. The Markhams might not be royalty, but at least they had a smattering of blue blood. And, more to the point, the dress would very likely find its way onto the society pages of one or two of the upmarket magazines.

Diana sighed. She wished the wedding were over and done with. Then she wouldn't have to deal with people like Rachel any more. The entire business was so unwieldy. It was like a sprawling theatrical production in which she had been assigned a leading role, but no one had even stopped to ask if she wanted it. She had enjoyed the engagement party; that had been private, just a few select friends. This was different. This seemed to be taking place for the benefit of everyone except her. The curtain was going up in a fortnight's time. The spectators would be watching her expectantly, their eyes brimming with well-wishing sentiment, but *she didn't know her lines*. All she could do was go through what she presumed were the motions, and hope that she got it right.

Not for the first time, she wished she were a natural show-off like her elder sister. Emma, who was already married, had revelled in all the attention. She still talked of her wedding as being the happiest day of her life, even though it had been six years ago. Diana sometimes suspected that Emma quite fancied getting a divorce, just so she could marry her husband all over again.

The music petered out. Rachel gestured across the

room for one of her assistants to turn the tape over. There were some mechanical clicks, a few halting chords, and then a woman began to sing.

The volume was low; the voice could only just be heard above the rustling and murmuring, but Diana thought she recognised the aria. She hummed along to it under her breath until the voice started hitting notes too high for her to follow, even in her imagination.

'Isn't this the one where she goes mad?' she wondered out loud, more to herself than to Rachel or any of the others.

'What's that?' asked Rachel, uninterested. Classical music bored her, but she thought it lent a touch of class to her fitting sessions.

'I can't remember the name of the opera,' Diana said. 'But I think she stabs her husband to death on their wedding night. It's terribly gory. There was blood all over her dress when they did it at Covent Garden.'

Rachel tutted. 'Well, I hope you're not thinking of treating Oliver like that,' she said. 'Though I suppose it might make a good newspaper story. Let's have something a little lighter, shall we?' She clapped her hands, calling for the tape to be changed once more.

Diana felt impatient. She'd been enjoying the music. She jerked her head round to watch the assistant at the tape deck. The sudden movement startled the apprentice seamstress. Her fingers slipped, and the sharp end of a pin jabbed into Diana's skin.

It wasn't much. Just a pinprick. Diana hardly felt it. She looked down to where a red droplet was glistening. It was just above the neckline of her dress.

It was such a tiny drop of blood. But, as Diana looked at it, the fitting-room receded into the distance. Its sounds suddenly seemed muffled by a thick layer of cotton wool. She started to shiver. She felt overwhelmingly drowsy. Everything was too much effort. She wanted to curl up and go to sleep on the couch. They could carry on sewing the dress without her.

It was like the fairytale. She would fall asleep for a hundred years. Oliver would have to wake her with a kiss. No, not Oliver: he'd be dead by then. But at least, that way, she'd miss the wedding.

The girl was stuttering her apologies, even though it had been Diana's fault. Rachel pushed her to one side and bent to inspect the damage.

'The dress!' she rasped. 'Watch it!' One of the seamstresses wiped the blood away, briskly, before it could turn to a trickle and stain the white satin.

*   *   *

Eight thousand miles away, in the departure lounge of Los Angeles International Airport, Jenny Hoffman flinched. She'd felt a small pricking sensation in her chest. It was so small, she'd hardly noticed it. But she did notice that she'd started to shiver, despite the warmth. There was a jacket draped over her shoulders. She drew it around her more tightly.

TUESDAY

It was morning. It was time to get up. Diana turned off the alarm and flopped back, exhausted. She gazed sightlessly at the ceiling. There was still so much to do.

Most of the time, she was so busy preparing for the wedding that there was no time to worry about it. She seemed to be spending half her time on the telephone, confirming reservations and chasing up the gasmen, who still hadn't fixed a date to come and connect the cooker. She argued with the electricians who were replacing the wiring on the upper floors of the house. She arranged for the delivery of crates. She placed orders for furniture and began to stock the kitchen cupboards with packets and tins. The flat would be ready for them when they got back from Venice, but only just.

She was looking forward to Venice. She'd bought a new suitcase and packed it with the kind of clothes she had never owned before: silk lingerie, stockings and a lace suspender belt, as well as a tight black dress which showed rather more leg than she was used to showing.

Oliver was being kept busy at the airbase, but once or twice he'd managed to slip away and give her a hand. She caught herself wishing they could spend more time together. But soon, she remembered, they would be together for ever. Soon they would have all the time in the world.

It wasn't all smooth sailing, but the hitches were minor ones. Diana felt herself swept up on a wave of goodwill. Everyone was being nice to her. Life was on automatic, and she just let it happen. This was how it was meant to be, she realised. This was what happened when you got married. She wasn't the first girl in the world to swap surnames, and she certainly wouldn't be the last. Everything was fine.

So why was she having nightmares?

Emma brought her a mug of tea. She sat up in bed and sipped it. This was the last time she'd be waking up in her sister's guest room. From now on, she'd be sleeping at the flat. On her own, of course. Oliver wouldn't be staying there until after the wedding.

She thought about the dream. It had seemed so *real*. She had gone through everyone, living all the details of the days leading up to the wedding: shopping and last-minute arrangements, phone calls and visits from friends.

And then, at the altar, she'd decided that she didn't want to marry Oliver after all.

He'd been furious. He'd struck her across the face, in front of everyone. She'd felt so embarrassed.

And then she'd been angry too. She'd hit him back. She'd hit him so hard that his head had fallen off. She'd been covered in blood.

And then the alarm had gone off. She'd woken up.

It had been horrible. Oliver had been so angry with her. And it had all been so realistic. She'd almost believed it was really happening. She'd had nightmares before, but never anything as bad as this.

Except for that one time. She thought about it now. It had been many years ago. She'd been about eight years old. She had dreamt about a place that was cold and damp. She was lying on the floor, face pressed against the wet concrete, unable to move. She shouted, but no one heard her. Her cries echoed uselessly back from the low, vaulted ceiling. It was dark, but she thought she could make out large shapes whirling on the edges of her vision. She hadn't felt frightened: just helpless and hopelessly lost. And sad. Very sad.

Her mother took the telephone call when it came the next day. They were in the town house. Diana had been looking forward to going to the cinema that afternoon, but the look on her mother's face immediately informed her that all treats were off.

'Diana,' her mother said. 'Your grandfather's had an accident.'

Mrs Markham blamed herself. They should never have come to town and left the old man alone in Hertfordshire. He'd gone down to the cellar for a bottle of claret. He'd slipped on the steps, broken his leg and several ribs in the fall. He was dead by the time the cleaning woman had found him the next morning.

'But I dreamt about it,' Diana sobbed.

'Yes, yes,' her mother said. 'Of course you did.' She smoothed her daughter's hair, near to tears herself.

Diana often wondered if she could have done something to save her grandfather. Suppose she had got up and told her mother as soon as she'd had the dream? They might have been able to get to him in time.

But there was something which frightened her even more than the thought of the old man lying on the basement floor as his life drained slowly away. She'd been angry with him when they'd left for town. He'd promised to take her to the zoo, but at the last minute he'd changed his mind. He wasn't coming with them, he'd decided to spend the weekend on his own.

Diana couldn't actually remember wishing he were dead, but she wasn't sure. She'd thrown a childish tantrum. She'd wished a lot of things that might have been better left unwished.

Suppose she had dreamt about the accident *before* it had happened? Suppose she had *made* it happen?

She'd never described the dream to anyone. Except Deborah, of course, many years later. Deborah had been quite excited by it. She'd made Diana go through every detail, again and again, until Diana had started to sulk with annoyance.

But then Deborah had always been fascinated by dreams. Especially Diana's. It was part of her job. What would she make of this latest one?

Diana examined her feelings. Of course she wanted to get married. She loved Oliver, didn't she? Of course she did. He was perfect, apart from his bad temper. No, she corrected herself. Oliver wasn't bad-tempered at all. That had been the dream. Oliver had the sweetest, kindest nature imaginable. She was lucky to have found him. He was almost too good to be true.

Diana thought about it. Wedding nerves. It had to be wedding nerves. And the best way to avoid them was to keep busy.

*   *   *

Jenny opened her eyes. Her mouth was dry Her limbs ached. There was a blanket tucked beneath her chin, but she still felt cold.

Hovering in front of her was a heavily powdered face, with a red mouth in the middle. The mouth opened, and words came out. It took Jenny a moment to work out what was being said. Her ears were bunged up and she couldn't hear properly.

'Time to wake up,' the mouth was saying. 'Please fasten your safety-belt. We're coming in to land.'

The stewardess moved along to the next row of seats. Jenny heard the instructions repeated.

She rubbed her eyes and yawned, trying to unblock

her ears. She'd been dreaming again: something about a girl in white, who had done something terrible and was screaming hysterically. Jenny had been watching, bemused, when an old man came up to her.

'You don't want to get mixed up in this,' he'd said. 'Go back, while there's still time.'

'But I *am* mixed up in it,' she'd protested.

The old man shook his head sorrowfully. Then he'd disappeared, and the rest of the dream had disappeared with him.

The sleep had done nothing for Jenny She felt even more wrecked now than before she'd dozed off. She fumbled for her trainers, trying to squeeze them onto swollen feet. There was a fluttering in the pit of her stomach that she knew was not entirely due to the drop in altitude. The dream had revived all her old doubts. She wished she'd stayed at home, except that she didn't know where home *was* any more. She wished she'd carried on with her life as though nothing had ever happened, as though there'd been no solicitor's letter telling her her aunt had died. Shit, she hadn't even known she'd *had* an aunt. That was bad enough, but the rest . . .

But it had happened. The letter had arrived. Her life, or what she had thought of as her life, was shattered. Nothing would ever be the same again. The choice was simple. Either she could pick up the pieces, go on as before, and maybe spend the rest of her life wondering. Or she could come to England. Dig up the facts. Face the truth.

It was too late to turn back now, even if she had really wanted to. Half of the unexpected windfall had already gone on the plane ticket. Chickening out now would be an unholy waste of cash. Anyway, everyone told her that London was a good place to be, especially for music. She could take in some clubs, go to a few gigs. It might be fun.

But, more than that, she had the uneasy feeling that wheels had been set in motion, that some sort of machinery was already grinding away. There were cogs missing, but it was up to her to provide them. Then everything would click into place, for better or worse.

Probably worse, Jenny thought. She wasn't superstitious, but she prided herself on a sort of positive pessimism. Better to be prepared for the worst than to hope for the best and be disappointed. The trouble was, she had no idea what the worst might turn out to be.

The plane swooped down to circle Heathrow. The pilot was waiting for the go-ahead to land. Jenny found herself wishing it would circle forever. She almost hoped it would crash. Then she wouldn't have to face up to whatever it was that was waiting for her down below.

Jenny Hoffman, she thought. You've been living a dream. Welcome to the Real World. *Come on down.*

* * *

Diana yawned as she drove back from the garden centre. She couldn't seem to stop yawning. She wished the feeling of drowsiness would go away. It was cold in the car, and the heater did nothing to warm the air. She wished she'd worn a heavier jacket, instead of this thin linen one. Her skin crawled with goose pimples.

There was a small forest of estate agents' boards planted outside the house. It looked a mess. The local council levied fines, but for every board that came down, another three or four went up. Diana edged her Renault into a parking space nearby and clambered out, pulling the carrier bags after her. Then she unloaded the box with the glossy *Monstera* and the rather droopy-looking *Chamaedorea elegans*. The palm would soon perk up, she thought, looking down at it fondly. She had a way with green things. Everyone told her so.

It was a shame about the flowerbed in front of the house. That would have to go. But then there would be room for a private parking space. She wouldn't always be able to park so easily around here. Especially during the cricket season, when people would be flocking to Lords and jamming the area with their cars.

They'd been lucky to find the house. Oliver had been rather picky about the other places, but he'd taken to this one immediately. Late Victorian, Diana's father had said as he'd presented her with the lease. Too big for one family, but solid, and ripe for conversion. They'd want to find somewhere else, of course. Selling off the other flats would eventually help pay for somewhere out of town. They could keep this flat on, if they liked, as a *pied-à-terre*. But London was no place for bringing up children.

Diana wedged the box against the front door and fumbled in her bag for the keys. She wasn't used to them yet. There were several false starts before she found the right one.

The hallway smelled of fresh plaster. There were three push-button switches along the wall, but only the nearest of the lightbulbs was working. She could hear faint scuffling noises overhead. The electricians were still fiddling around upstairs. They would have to fix the lights before the other people moved in.

It was all right for her, though. The nearest lightbulb, the one that worked, hung right outside her door. And during the day she didn't need to turn it on anyway. The house faced west. Afternoon light slanted through the amber pane in the hallway. But, further back, the hallway kinked. The staircase leading to the other apartments lay in shadow, and the area near the back door was even murkier.

Diana fiddled with the keys, trying to remember which was which. Two mortices and one Yale later, the door to her flat swung inwards. This would be where Oliver was supposed to scoop her in his arms and carry her over the threshold.

She had been here a few times already. It was already beginning to feel like home, despite the packing cases all over the place. It wasn't her first flat, but it was the first one she wouldn't be sharing with anyone. Well, she'd be sharing it with Oliver, but that was different.

It wasn't enormous, but it would do nicely until they found time for some serious house-hunting. Diana envisaged a Georgian cottage (four bedrooms at least) where she could potter happily in the garden. The children could wait, at least until she'd got the landscaping sorted out.

She went through into the kitchen and deposited the plants on the table. The cooker was waiting to be connected, but the fridge was already purring softly. There were still some gaps in the fittings. One of Diana's uncles had promised them a dishwasher, and Oliver's parents were going to cough up for a washing machine. Diana had never thought of herself as a housewife, somehow. She tried to imagine what it would be like loading and unloading piles of Oliver's dirty underwear. She supposed she would get used to it. She could always hire a home-help if the going got tough.

The daylight was fading fast. Diana felt the radiator. It was cold. She steeled herself for a confrontation with the thermostat. The instructions were taped to the wall: set the timer, align the arrows, press the knob, hold it down and *turn slowly*. Oliver had demonstrated the process three times, very patiently, for her benefit, but Diana had never had much success with technical things. There was a click, followed by a mechanical splutter and a brief rumbling.

Diana unpacked one of her bags. Milk and butter joined the bottles in the fridge. Then she felt the radiator again. It was still cold. She ran water out of the hot tap. It was freezing.

'Damn and blast,' she snapped out loud.

It was all right, she thought. She knew what to do now. Oliver had shown her. But it wasn't all right really, because it meant she would have to go down into the basement.

Diana had never liked basements. She thought that perhaps it had something to do with her grandfather's death, but basements had always spooked her. Not so long ago, when her flatmates had gone out and left her alone, she had watched part of a TV movie. Each time the woman in the film had gone down into the basement, there had been a burst of *oooh-whee-oooh* music to denote something nasty lurking there. Diana had never found out what the something was. The film had frightened her so much that she'd switched the television off.

In a way, she wished she'd watched it through to the end, because whatever had been down there could hardly have been worse than her own vague imaginings. As it was, she had been plagued with nightmares for a while: nightmares in which she would be chased down into a basement and along dark subterranean passages. She never knew what was chasing her, but it made chuckling, squelching noises. She would always wake up before it caught her. Then she would lie there in the dark, too frightened to go back to sleep.

Sometimes she suspected the only reason she was marrying Oliver was because then there would be someone there, next to her in the bed, when she woke up in the dark after a bad dream. Of course, that wasn't the *only* reason she was marrying him, but still . . . She wondered how many people got married simply because they were afraid of the dark.

At first she'd wanted to take one of the apartments on the upper floors. The ground level felt insecure, somehow, even with locks on all the windows – too accessible to burglars and prowlers. But the other apartments were still being modernised. They wouldn't be ready in time for the wedding.

And anyway, Oliver had told her not to be so silly. The doors were fitted with deadlocks. He had shown her how to work the window latches with a small bolt release which he had put on the mantelpiece. 'There,' he had said. 'No one can get in. And if there's ever a fire, you'll know how to get out.'

As for the basement, Oliver had promised to clear it out as soon as he got the time. Mr Markham had talked of converting it into another flat, but there were insurmountable damp problems. And anyway, Diana didn't like to think of anyone living down there. She had visions of a huge family crammed into a tiny space, children pale and stunted from the lack of natural light, growing up to hate her father, the evil landlord who kept them in Dickensian squalor.

Oliver's idea was that the basement should be converted into something useful. They could paint it white, install a mini-gym, or fix up the broken pool table that was already down there, propped on its side. 'No problem,' he had said. 'Ghosts don't like sports.'

She had laughed. He was right. Spooks and sport didn't mix, somehow.

But the basement was pretty spooky, all the same. The entrance was under the stairs, by the back door. Diana crossed the hallway and went in.

She felt the temperature drop by several degrees. The climate was different in there – cold and damp. There was a barred window at the top of the stairs. But the glass, caked with dirt, let in only just enough light for her to see the steps descending into the dark.

She flicked the light switch. The low-watt bulb didn't do much more than throw a ring of light around the boiler below. Beyond it, rearing up out of the gloom, were piles of old furniture and stacks of boxes; enough junk to furnish several flats. Not all of it was broken, but it was shabby and antiquated: not to Diana's taste at all. A network of pipes and cables cast odd shadows against the outlines of low, brick-lined recesses. There were cobwebs down there, and probably spiders. *And even rats*, Diana thought. *Or worse.*

She made her way carefully down the stairs, keeping a hand against the wall for balance. Anyone taking a tumble and breaking a leg might lie down there for days. There would be no one to hear if she shouted for help. Unless the electricians happened to be around.

She went over to the boiler, looked behind it to check there was nothing lurking there. Then she opened the small panel in its front. As she had suspected, the pilot light was out. The valve was screwed tightly towards the 'off' sign. Those blasted electricians had shut it down, even though she had asked them not to. They took no notice of anything she said. She would have to get Oliver to have a word with them.

She twisted the valve. Nothing happened. There was a box of kitchen matches on the ledge nearby. The box felt damp to the touch, but she managed to get one of the matches going on the third strike. She held it to the element for a moment. The thin blue flame flickered in the draught from the stairs, but it didn't go out.

There, Diana thought. That hadn't been so difficult, had it? Feeling rather proud of herself, she turned back towards the steps . . .

. . . and saw something moving on the edge of the shadows.

She made herself stand still and look. There was nothing there, of course. Only a stack of old tea-chests and cardboard cartons. She was tired. Her eyes were playing odd little tricks on her.

But she *had* seen something after all. Sticking out from one of the cartons was a tiny foot.

Diana's instincts told her to go straight back upstairs. But she remembered the film she had watched on TV. She wasn't too keen on knowing there was a tiny foot down here, and not knowing what the tiny foot was attached to.

She made herself move in for a closer look. The foot was perfectly formed, but she could see straight away that it was too tiny to belong to a human being. She was relieved at that. Probably some sort of puppet, she thought. The lid of the box was already hanging off. She pulled it aside to find a stack of old picture frames, a chipped plaster-of-Paris poodle, half-wrapped in discoloured tissue paper, and an assortment of ashtrays, some of them self-proclaimed souvenirs of various European cities. Diana decided that whoever had lived here previously had had the most ghastly taste in ornaments.

The foot was attached to a leg, and the leg was attached to something still buried in the clutter. Diana scrabbled around and pulled out a large doll. It was dressed in the yellowing remains of what might once have been a wedding gown. The craftsmanship was exquisite: the arms and legs were perfectly scaled-down copies of human limbs. The figure was jointed so that it could be bent at the knees, elbows, neck and waist. It was very old, possibly antique. It had probably started life propped up on someone's mantelpiece. It was certainly not the sort of doll you bought for little girls to cuddle, Diana thought. It was too fragile; the cream-coloured porcelain had cracked in one or two places. One of the cracks snaked across the left side of the doll's face. She peered closer. The face wore a slightly smug expression, and the crack made its features look vaguely oriental. The cheeks were very round, the eyebrows arched like Joan Crawford's, and the lips were painted in a perfect crimson Cupid's bow. Diana didn't think it was a very pretty doll, but she felt sorry for it. It had probably been down here for years, waiting in its wedding dress for a bridegroom who never came. Diana swivelled one of its arms and examined the tiny fingers on each hand. She peered closer. Each tiny finger had a tiny pointed fingernail, and each tiny pointed fingernail had an even tinier half-moon, and each . . .

The boiler ignited with a *whoosh*.

Diana jumped, almost dropping the doll. She'd forgotten where she was or what she was meant to be doing. She certainly didn't want to hang around in the basement any longer than was necessary. She went back upstairs. She didn't have the heart to leave the doll lying down in the basement on its own. She took it with her.

* * *

The desk clerk looked her up and down, his mouth pinched in a prim expression of disapproval. Good grief. There were *words* on her T-shirt. He could make out the letters KEFIN and RIP, but her jacket hid the rest. Probably just as well, he thought. It was probably some sociopathic slogan which would shock the resident geriatrics and send them scuttling to the porter to complain. The desk clerk stared at the jacket. There were studs on it. It looked like a biker's jacket. It looked as though an entire chapter of Hell's Angels had ridden their bikes over it – several times.

She was wearing jeans, too. They were scruffy enough, but at least they weren't denim. Only yesterday a youth in Levis had been ejected from the tearoom. The hotel had its standards, after all. The clerk enjoyed seeing people being kicked out. Served them right if they didn't know how to dress.

He could easily have sent this one packing, but she had a reservation. He asked her for a larger deposit than was necessary. She supplied it without a qualm, counting it out from a wad of notes drawn from her inside pocket. Probably stolen, the clerk thought as she handed it over.

He dumped her key on the counter where she had to stretch to reach it. The light caught her head as she leant forward. The clerk saw to his disgust that her hair was not black, as he had first supposed, but black with blue highlights. And her earlobes were pierced in several places. There was a small skull-and-crossbones dangling from one of the holes. The clerk winced. If only he'd seen that earlier, he thought. He might have been able to fob her off with some excuse about the room being double-booked. She wouldn't like it here anyway. She didn't fit in. The next-youngest guests were old enough to be her grandparents.

'Thanks, dude,' she said. 'Have a nice day!' She flashed a grin that left the desk clerk quailing in indignation. *Asshole*, she thought, picking up her bags.

She reached the lift just as an elderly couple emerged from behind its doors. The woman had a blue-rinsed perm. She muttered something to her husband, who stared angrily at Jenny as she passed. *Fellow countrymen*, she thought.

She pressed the button for the fourth floor, and shivered. London was like Antarctica. Or maybe it was just something walking over her grave. She hadn't felt warm since leaving Los Angeles. She decided to shop for a sweater in the morning.

The foyer had been misleading. It had been designed to give the impression of art deco elegance. Behind it, the rest of the hotel was decked out in functional facelessness. International hotel style, Jenny surmised, as soon as she saw the bland, streamlined furnishing of her room. The accent was on cheap veneer. She surveyed the orange bedspread and curtains with distaste. She might as well have gone to a Holiday Inn back home.

A faint hiss of street noise filtered through the double glazing. The view was nothing to write home about, but at least she'd managed to pick a place in the centre of town. It would be easy to get around from here.

She set her bags down, switched on the television and flicked through the channels impatiently. *Jeezus*, she thought. Only four channels. And nothing but talking heads on any of them.

She flopped onto the bed, fished a packet of cigarettes from her pocket and lit one up. Then she uncapped her duty-free vodka and took a swig from it. She pulled the London street atlas out of its paper bag. She began to study the index and maps.

Occasionally, she took a look at the television screen, where two men were conducting a heated argument. One of the men was fat and the other thin. At first she thought they must be comedians, but they didn't seem to be telling jokes. Jenny didn't think they were funny, anyway. But then, she knew, the English had a weird sense of humour.

*   *   *

The programme was so boring that Diana hardly noticed when it ended. It was only when the screen evaporated into a black and white fog that she realised she'd been dozing off again. There was a late-night movie on one of the other channels, but it looked as though it might turn out to be frightening. She didn't want to get spooked, not on her first night alone in the flat. She switched the set off and curled up on the sofa with a copy of *Harpers & Queen*. The diary pages, as usual, were full of vaguely familiar faces. Diana yawned and checked her watch. If Oliver didn't call soon, she'd be asleep.

*   *   *

Jenny didn't have a whole lot of unpacking to do, but she hadn't got very far with it. Clothes lay in an untidy heap on the armchair, but her hold-all was only half empty. She was curled up on the orange bedspread, the open street atlas face-down beside her. The television screen fizzed with static. Her last cigarette had burnt down to a small grey cylinder in the ashtray.

The telephone began to buzz. Automatically she stretched out a hand to answer it. 'Hi,' she mumbled, half-asleep.

'Miss Hoffman? There's a call for you.'

'Thanks,' she said. There was a nagging thought at the back of her brain but she was too sleepy to deal with it now. Back in LA, she thought, they'd just be waking up. She heard a clicking on the line.

'Hello?' said a voice. It sounded long-distance. 'Jenny? We trust you had a comfortable journey.'

'Yeah. Who is this?' Jenny asked, rubbing her eyes.

There was more clicking, and then the voice said: 'Just checking the line. Nothing wrong with the connection. You can go ahead now.'

'What?' said Jenny. But the phone went dead.

It was only when she'd replaced the receiver that the nagging thought crystallised. She'd left no forwarding address. People knew she was in London, okay. But no one knew she was here.

Assholes from the telephone company, she thought, reaching out for another shot of vodka. They must be working overtime.

*   *   *

Diana opened her eyes. She'd forgotten to draw the curtains. Orange sodium from the streetlights was filtering into the room. She was curled up, fully dressed, on the sofa. It wasn't terribly comfortable. She shifted her

23

position and found herself gazing into the face of the porcelain doll. She couldn't think what it was doing there. She thought she'd left it in the kitchen.

Something had woken her up. She thought she'd heard someone talking. They'd stopped now, though. Now there was nothing but the irregular hum of distant traffic.

And . . . something else. She twisted her head to look round the room. Everything was still and silent in the half-light. Her teddybear gazed at her mournfully from the armchair, hurt at having been ousted by the upstart doll. *Poor Melrose*, she thought. He needs a hug.

She heard it again. It was a soft noise, so soft that she might have imagined it. It sounded like the cracking of eggshells. The doll stared sightlessly at her, and she stared back. Surely its face was a different shape?

No, she thought, she'd been imagining things.

And then she noticed that the crack had been spreading, forking into tiny tributaries across the doll's face. The porcelain was now covered by a network of fine black veins.

She prodded the face with her finger; the finely crazed surface felt smooth to the touch. But there was one piece of china which looked loose. She inserted the edge of a fingernail into the crack and prised the chip away. It was a satisfying feeling, like peeling a hardboiled egg. Unable to stop herself, she pulled off another flake, and then another, until she'd peeled half of a cheek away.

She peered into the hole she had made. There was something inside the doll's head. It looked like soggy cotton wool. Greyish-white. She pulled away more of the fine china flakes. Then, very gingerly, she inserted the tip of her finger into the hole.

She didn't like what she felt at all. The greyish-white stuff was soft. She snatched her finger away. She could have sworn she had felt something pulse beneath her touch.

There was a sound like milk seeping into breakfast cereal. The cheek disintegrated. Inside the head, something uncoiled. It might have been a fat white wine gum. A tiny, glistening tip nosed through the remaining shards of porcelain, like a crocus pushing its way into the sunlight. It poised there in the air, groping blindly.

Diana leapt to her feet with a strangled shout, shoving the doll away from her. It fell face down on the floor. Frantically, she wiped her hand on her skirt. She had *touched* it. Whatever it was, she had actually *touched* it. Her skin crawled with revulsion. She looked around for something to grab: a newspaper or magazine. She had to kill it. Whatever it was, she had to kill it.

Her foot squelched down on something soft. Feeling sick, she looked down. The maggot was wriggling feebly in its own juices. Half of its body had been flattened into a translucent grey ooze which was sinking slowly into the carpet. The *new* carpet, Diana thought, groaning inwardly. It had only just been fitted.

She wanted it off her floor. She would get a J-cloth and disinfectant from the kitchen, wipe all trace of it away. She looked suspiciously at the squashed jelly, but it didn't seem capable of crawling anywhere. Keeping it in her sights for as long as possible, she backed out of the room.

She paused outside the kitchen door, listening. She hadn't been mistaken after all. She *could* hear voices. Someone was in there. A little hesitantly, she opened the door and took a step inside.

Someone said: 'But that road's closed to traffic. Unless we get another driver, that is.'

Her surprise turned to relief. It was Oliver, and he was here with his parents. They were sitting around the kitchen table, drinking coffee. He hadn't bothered to phone, after all. He had come straight round.

'It's all in the bag,' he was saying. 'Angela's got it all under control.'

'Oliver!' she said, starting towards him. 'Thank goodness you're here. There's the most revolting . . .'

She drew up short. All heads had swivelled in her direction. They were all staring at her. They didn't look pleased to see her *at all*.

Then Mrs Hall wrinkled her face and turned away in disgust. 'Well, *really*,' she said.

Oliver stood up. He looked absolutely furious.

Diana wondered if she had interrupted a family argument. But no, he was angry with *her*. What on earth had she done now?

There was something wrong here. She suddenly realised that she felt cold. The air was very cold on her skin. On *all* of her skin. Even before she had cast her eyes down to her body, she realised with a sinking feeling what it was that was wrong.

She was completely naked. No, not quite naked, she thought, foolishly. *Worse* than naked. She had on a flimsy white suspender belt. One stocking was dragging at it. The other was bunched in a silk concertina around her ankle. And she was carrying a small bouquet. Stephanotis, she thought, catching a whiff of the aroma. She tried, without much success, to cover herself up with the flowers.

'But you said she was a virgin!' Mr Hall exclaimed. 'She doesn't look like a virgin to me. She looks like a slut.'

Oliver strode towards her, knocking a chair out of the way as he advanced. 'Good God, Diana! What the hell do you think you're playing at? How *dare* you behave like this in front of my parents?'

Before she knew what was happening, he had hit her, quite sharply, across the face. She stumbled backwards, tears springing to her eyes. It wasn't fair. It wasn't her fault. They hadn't told her they were coming. Filled with embarrassment, she turned and fled.

She ran into the bedroom. She span round in a panic, trying to find her dressing-gown. It was nowhere to be seen. Oliver came after her. She turned to face him. She could explain everything. But he hit her again. The impact knocked her sideways.

There was a smile on his face now. It was a curiously twisted smile, and there seemed to be too many teeth in it. She'd never seen him look like that before. He didn't look like Oliver at all.

'No!' she started to shout, but he clamped his hand over her mouth and pushed her roughly back onto the bed. Then he was on her, pinning her arms to the pillow with one of his hands.

He brought his face down very close to hers. Diana could smell something on his breath. Whisky, she thought it might have been, but she wasn't sure. It could have been something else.

'This is just child's play,' he whispered very softly. 'Angela's fed up with toys. Soon we'll be getting down to the *real thing*. We don't get many virgins around here, you know. They're hard to come by these days. We almost had one once, but she got away . . .'

'Oliver,' she pleaded. 'What's got into you?'

'I'll show you what's got into me,' he said.

He opened his mouth wide. So wide that she thought he was going to swallow the room, and her with it. She saw his tongue uncoiling, feeling its way through the air towards her. It was black and pointed, not like a normal tongue at all. She stared at it, horrified, as it flickered in front of her. He made a high-pitched noise in the back of his throat.

Then she closed her eyes. She didn't want to see any more.

His weight was lifted from her quite suddenly, as though he had been snatched into the air. Diana threw herself off the bed. She felt something scrunch beneath one of her heels as she landed in a crouch on the floor.

Oh no, she thought. *Not again*. She looked down.

She'd landed on the doll. Half its face was gone. Pieces of china littered the floor around her feet. There was no sign of the oozing maggot.

There never had *been* an oozing maggot. Diana searched the carpet. It was completely unmarked. She'd been sleeping, fully-clothed, on the sofa.

Oh God, she'd been *dreaming* again.

There was an unfamiliar shrilling sound. Diana looked at the telephone. It was the first time she had heard it ring.

She took a deep breath. And picked up the receiver.

'Diana?'

'Oliver,' she said. 'Is it really you? You're not angry?'

'It's a wretched line, darling. You'll have to speak up.'

'Where . . . where are you?'

'Sorry I didn't ring earlier, darling. I just got back.'

'Y . . . yes . . .' Diana's voice trailed off. She was still trembling.

'Are you all right? You sound a bit odd.'

'Yes, I'm fine.' She didn't feel fine at all. 'I just fell asleep on the sofa. I think I was dreaming . . .'

'About me, I hope!'

'Yes, but . . .'

'Hope I didn't wake you.'

'Oliver, I . . .'

'Listen, I can hardly hear you, darling. I've got to go now, but I'll call you back in the morning. Sleep tight. Keep dreaming about me. Bye now.'

Diana said goodbye. There was a faint click, and the dialling tone started up.

She stared at her hands. One of her fingernails was torn and jagged. The polish was chipped. She crossed to the mirror over the mantelpiece. Her face was shiny with perspiration. Her hair looked lank and greasy. She looked dreadful.

WEDNESDAY

Diana felt a wave of nostalgia sweep over her as she approached the school. It wasn't so much that she had enjoyed the job. She liked children, but what she missed most was the day-to-day dealing with uncomplicated human beings. Kids hadn't had time to develop all the odd little tics that made grown-ups so difficult. Everyone was such hard work. Everyone expected her to behave like a spoilt little rich girl, and they felt cheated when she didn't. At least, she *hoped* she didn't behave like that. She tried not to.

The only person she could think of who wasn't hard work was Oliver. Oliver accepted her for what she was, not for what he thought she ought to be. Perhaps she would tell him about the nightmares after all.

She parked the car and walked up to the gates. It was early afternoon, and yet parents were already waiting outside. No, she corrected herself as she drew closer. These men didn't look like the sort of parents whose children would be attending the school. In fact, they didn't appear to be parents at all. She didn't like the look of them. She didn't know why. She just didn't.

One of the men was grossly overweight. Greasy strips of hair were plastered across his skull in a pathetic effort to disguise encroaching baldness. The other man was tall and thin, with eyebrows that met in the middle over a beaked nose. They looked like a couple of TV comedians,

29

the sort who would tell off-colour jokes. They were peering through the railings at the empty yard that served as a playground during breaks. They looked, Diana decided, like child molesters. She made a mental note to warn Miss Daley. Just in case. One couldn't be too careful these days.

'Miss Markham?'

The thin man had seen her and was striding in her direction. How did he know her name? She paused by the gates and turned on the automatic smile she kept for such occasions, racking her brains to think where she might have seen him before. She didn't want to seem rude. They must have been introduced at some time, and she had forgotten. She was always being introduced to people.

Now the fat man had also seen her. He was bobbing in the thin man's wake, pointing something towards her. There was a mechanical whirring and a flash of light that left her blinking, and she realised it was a camera.

The thin man reached her. He grabbed one of her hands and pumped it enthusiastically as he introduced himself. 'Paul Lawrence,' he said. '*West London Post and Echo*. Pleased to meet you, Miss Markham.'

He smiled, revealing a row of evenly-spaced teeth. Diana found the effect more creepy than charming. He reminded her of a storybook wolf.

The fat man wasn't to be outdone. 'Peck,' he said.

'What?' said Diana.

'My name,' said the fat man. 'It's *Peck*.'

Diana couldn't have cared less what his name was. She had never met these men before and she didn't particularly feel like talking to them. She wished they would say whatever it was they wanted to say and leave her alone.

'I wonder if you'd mind answering a few questions,' the thin man said.

'Me?' Diana blinked as the fat man took another photograph. 'I'm afraid you must have mistaken me for someone else.' She backed away from them, slightly alarmed now. 'Thanks awfully, but I've got to go. I'm late . . .'

The thin man stepped in front of her. 'No mistake, Miss Markham. We'd like to run a feature on you, if you don't mind. About you and your fiancé. Oliver Hall, isn't it? You're big news, you know.'

'What kind of feature?' asked Diana. She flinched as the flashgun popped again. 'Please stop that,' she said to the fat man, who was poking his zoom lens in her face.

'Oh, you know,' the thin man said. 'A nice bit of romance for the punters. "The War Hero and the Debutante". That sort of thing. "From the blood-spattered battlefields of Port Stanley to the posh drawing-rooms of Knightsbridge."'

'But I don't even live in Knightsbridge,' Diana protested.

He didn't seem to have heard her. 'It's the contrast that'll get 'em going,' he said. 'I mean, one minute he's up to his arse in mud and shit . . .'

'Throttling Argies with his bare hands!' the fat man cried.

'. . . And now here he is, hobnobbing with high society! Marrying into the nobility! We want the inside story. What we want to know is, how does it *feel*?'

'I beg your pardon?' Diana was totally confused. They must still be thinking she was someone else.

'How does it *feel* to get between the sheets with a bloke who's been given a chestful of gongs for killing wops? What do *you* think about it? We want the inside story. How does it *feel*?'

'Please go away!' said Diana. She felt her face go red with annoyance. How could she have been stupid enough to stop and talk to these awful people? She darted past the thin man and through the open gate, slamming it

31

shut in his face. He made no attempt to follow her.

It was best to ignore them, she thought, striding as briskly as she could towards the door. She didn't look back, but she could still feel their eyes drilling into her back. Just as she reached the safety of the doorway, she heard voices, no doubt raised for her benefit.

'I know what *she* wants,' one of them said.

'Yeah,' said the other. 'Silly stuck-up bitch.'

It wasn't *fair*, Diana thought. And then she shut the door.

*   *   *

'Don't worry about it,' Deborah said. Diana had told her about the reporters. She was still trembling with anger.

They were sitting by the window in Miss Daley's office. Outside, two children were locked in a wrestling hold. One of them was squealing. Deborah shifted the mug of tea to her left hand and rapped sharply on the glass. The children looked up, and the bigger of the two loosed his grip. The victim gratefully slipped out of his grasp and ran off.

'William's turning out to be rather a bully,' said Deborah. 'It's that father of his, I suppose. Too much emphasis on discipline. People are terrified of showing affection these days. They're all terrified their kids are going to turn into heroin addicts.'

'I'm a bit on edge, I suppose,' Diana said. 'Normally it wouldn't bother me at all.'

'Well, there's bound to be a certain amount of interest from the press,' said Deborah, still gazing out into the playground. 'You'll have to learn how to deal with it. But you mustn't let it get to you.'

'I just can't wait for the wedding to be over,' said Diana. 'I should be looking forward to it, but I'm not. I'm dreading it.'

Deborah tore her gaze away from the window and directed her full attention towards Diana, who felt a little uncomfortable under the sudden scrutiny.

'It's only natural that you should feel nervous,' said Deborah. 'It wouldn't be normal if you didn't.' She must have realised that her tone was a little too businesslike, because she softened it. 'How are you feeling? You look tired. Still sleeping badly?'

Diana nodded. 'I can't seem to get a decent night's rest. The nightmares are getting worse.'

Deborah inclined her head to one side. For a moment, Diana felt a twinge of annoyance. Why couldn't Deborah drop the professional façade, and just treat her as a friend? All she needed was someone to talk to. She didn't need a psychoanalyst, for heaven's sake! Then the moment passed, and she felt guilty at having thought such things. Deborah was only trying to help, after all.

'If only those bastards hadn't cut off my grant,' Deborah was saying. 'I was really getting somewhere with that dream research, you know. I wish you'd come to see me then. Particularly with what you've told me about the dreams you had as a child. The premonitions.'

'These dreams aren't premonitions,' Diana retorted. 'You can't tell me that Oliver's really going to start hitting me around. That's ridiculous.'

'No, of course not,' said Deborah. 'That's too literal an interpretation. But you seem to have a peculiarly vivid recollection of your . . . nocturnal fantasies. That's very unusual, you know.'

'Not all the time,' Diana protested.

'Well, let's just say that your rate of recall is way above most people's,' Deborah said. 'And the content of your dreams is very . . . interesting.'

'Freudian, you mean,' Diana said, sticking her chin out. 'I suppose it's all to do with Oliver. The trouble is, I can't work out whether it's the bad dreams that are

33

making me edgy about the wedding, or worry about the wedding that's giving me bad dreams in the first place.'

'Cause or symptom, eh?' said Deborah. She lit a cigarette and paused for thought. Diana watched the smoke curl into the air.

'Dreaming,' Deborah continued, 'is merely the brain's way of confronting our subconscious fears and anxieties. You've come to a crucial stage in your adult development. Marriage is a big step for anyone to take. You should think of your nightmares as a healthy release.'

'*Healthy?*' Diana exclaimed. 'You really think this sounds normal?' She described what she could remember of her latest nightmare to Deborah, who nodded sagely as she listened.

'Classic stuff,' she said, when Diana told her about stepping on the maggot. 'Like in *Eraserhead*.'

Diana looked puzzled. 'I don't know about that,' she said. 'But it was pretty yucky. Anyway, *then* I went into the kitchen . . .' When it came to the part about Oliver throwing her onto the bed, she faltered.

Deborah nodded again. 'It's nothing to worry about,' she said kindly.

'He's so different in my dreams,' said Diana. 'He's always angry with me. And he's rough. Not at all like the Ollie I know.'

'And what does Oliver have to say about this?'

'I don't know,' Diana replied. 'I haven't told him.'

'You want him to think you're perfect,' said Deborah, smiling to herself. 'No, no, that's okay. A nice girl with no complications, no kinky subtext. Men like that sort of thing.'

'It's not so much that,' Diana said. 'It's just that it all sounds so silly in the cold light of day.'

'It's not silly at all,' Deborah said. 'Listen, I don't think you should worry so much about what Oliver thinks. Oliver can take care of himself. I've known him for longer than you have. And, believe me, Oliver can take care of himself.'

Diana sighed. 'But he's so sweet. And I feel so guilty about having made him into some sort of bogeyman.'

'It seems to me,' said Deborah, 'that you're not dreaming about Oliver at all. He's just a symbol.'

'A symbol? For what?'

Deborah shrugged slightly. 'Oh, it could be any number of things. He could be representative of parental authority, for instance. Every little girl harbours ambivalent feelings towards her father. She loves him, but she's also a little bit scared of him. She even wishes he were dead, on occasion. And she feels guilty about her feelings. In a way, every man she meets is a father substitute. And all the old fears and desires come bubbling up to the surface.'

'Do you really think so?' Diana asked doubtfully. She had never thought about her relationship with her father as anything other than straightforward. He was just her father. She loved him, but she didn't want to *marry* him. And she wasn't scared of him, either. Only when he was angry, and he hadn't been angry with her for a long time now. Not since she'd spilled orange juice all over some papers in his study.

'I'm sure of it,' said Deborah. 'You're about to take on a lot of new responsibilities. But first, your subconscious has to cope with all those old feelings of dependency that were nurtured within you as a child. We don't turn into adults overnight, you know. There is always a transitory stage, when the subconscious mind learns to interrelate with people as individuals instead of as symbols of authority. It's a complicated process.'

It certainly was. 'So I should just . . . lie back and let it happen?' Diana suggested. She was no longer sure what they were talking about.

'More or less,' said Deborah, stubbing out her cigarette.

'Why don't you buy yourself a book on dream psychology? It would help you to work out all the symbolism for yourself.' She checked her watch. 'I have to finish up here and get back to the clinic.' She patted Diana on the shoulder. 'There's nothing to worry about, Diana. Honestly.'

'I just wish I could get a decent night's sleep,' said Diana. 'I feel so tired all the time.'

Deborah stood up. 'Look, if it gets *really* bad, let me know and I'll prescribe something. As a last resort, mind. It's better to let your subconscious work things out for itself. There's nothing to worry about, really there isn't. Everything's going to be fine.'

Diana almost believed her.

'Oh,' Deborah added, almost as an afterthought. 'And you shouldn't let people push you around.'

Did she really let them do that, Diana asked herself?

'And don't take them at face value,' Deborah said. 'You're far too trusting, you know.'

And then she was gone. Diana was left with her thoughts. She looked out of the window. The small boy, the one who had been trapped in a headlock earlier on, had now got his tormentor down on the ground and was pummelling him mercilessly.

* * *

Paul Lawrence watched as Peck shovelled food into his mouth with a plastic fork. It was quite some spectacle. He watched, and he listened, because the shovelling was accompanied by a great deal of noise.

'You're disgusting,' he said to Peck, not without a certain degree of admiration.

'Takes years of practice,' Peck replied through a mouthful of noodles. 'I went to finishing school. Like Miss Fancy-Pants back there.'

'Just watch what you're doing, okay?' Paul picked pieces of beansprout off the car seat and deposited them in the ashtray. 'I only had this cleaned last week.'

'What time d'you reckon she'll be back?' asked Peck, gesturing with his fork so that sauce dripped onto the gear lever.

'Soon, I hope.' Paul looked over at the house. His mouth twisted into a sneer. 'So daddy bought us that for our wedding present, did he? Jesus H. Christ. It's all right for some. We're in the wrong business, Peck my old son.'

'Makes you want to puke,' said Peck.

'Yeah well, make sure you do it out the window, okay?'

'I wouldn't mind landing a tart like that myself,' Peck said through another mouthful. 'D'you reckon she'd marry *me* if I asked?'

'Yeah,' said Paul, watching the noodles slide down Peck's chin. 'You're just her type. Nice manners. Gourmet tastes. Good physique.'

'Generous in the salami department,' said Peck.

They both snickered.

* * *

Diana felt more cheerful as she drove back to the house. There was nothing to worry about. Everything was going to be fine. Deborah had told her so.

And Deborah knew what she was talking about. Diana's worries were small beer compared to some of the problems Deborah had been dealing with recently. She only ever spoke of them as hypothetical cases, of course. Deborah did what she could, but some of the children never got over their terrible experiences. They woke up screaming from nightmares that made Diana's bad dreams seem like light entertainment. She was thankful that her own upbringing had been so *ordinary*.

37

She took the corner into her road. Cars lined the street, but there was a small parking space about a hundred yards away from the house. Diana squeezed her car into it, feeling purposeful and efficient. All *right*, she thought. There was no time to worry about things going bump in the night. There were still a hundred and one odd jobs for her to do; she would deal with each day in a businesslike manner, and let the nightmares look after themselves.

Her positive frame of mind didn't last very long. It began to crack as soon as she got out of the car and, stooping to collect her handbag, caught sight of the far side of the street. Another car door was opening. Out of the corner of her eye, as she walked towards the house, she saw Paul Lawrence and Peck spill out into the road and come hurrying after her, although Peck didn't so much spill as *ooze*. He was a walking dollop of protozoan slime.

Her heart sank. Why couldn't they leave her in peace? She hadn't done anything to deserve this. She ducked her head and quickened her pace, hoping against hope that they'd leave her alone.

They caught up with her just as she reached the house. The thin man blocked her path with experienced ease. The fat one pointed his camera in her face, deliberately blinding her with his flash.

'Go away or I'll get the police,' she said, trying to sound calm.

'Come on, love, just a few questions,' the journalist wheedled. 'How did he pop the question? How did your father react to the news? Where are you going for the honeymoon? Who's doing the dress? Who's going to be at the wedding?'

'Stop it!' said Diana. She attempted to dodge past him, but he stepped sideways, spreading his arms. She fell back, not wanting him to touch her.

'Don't be shy, darling. We're just trying to do our jobs.'

'Yeah,' added the photographer. 'The public has a right to know.'

'A right to know *what*?' Diana sighed.

'Is he any good at it?' Paul Lawrence hunched forward till his face was only inches away from hers. His breath smelled bad.

'Yeah,' said the photographer. 'How big is his wanger?'

'His *what*?'

'His wanger, darling! His schlong, ding-a-ling, slasher, mutton cutlass, porksword, pecker! His *beef bayonet*?' The fat man was almost drooling. Now he winked at her.

Diana was confused. Was he swearing? Or talking about food, or what? 'I don't know *what* you're going on about,' she said angrily. 'Just leave me alone. Let me pass, please.'

'My goodness,' said the thin man, feigning surprise. 'You really don't know, do you? Peck, my old son, we've got a right one here.'

Diana felt tears welling up in her eyes. *Don't you dare cry*, she told herself sternly. *That's just what they'd like you to do*.

'You're still a virgin, aren't you?' leered the thin man.

She stared at him, open-mouthed. So that was it. They were talking about her sex life. She might have known it. She felt herself blushing.

'That's none of your business!' she blurted. 'How dare you!'

'So you deny it!' Paul Lawrence said gleefully. 'All right. We'll print that.'

'Print that and I'll sue!' Diana shouted. She would too. Her father had once sued *Private Eye*.

The photographer chortled. 'Nice one, Paulie. I can see the headline already. "The Deb Who Does It. Sexy Capers in the Kensington Smart Set."'

39

'But I don't *live* in Kensington!' Diana yelled, stamping her foot. She felt trapped. She had to get past them.

Without thinking, she swung at Paul Lawrence with her handbag.

He sidestepped easily. 'Oooh,' he said. 'So she wants to play rough, does she?' He launched into a mocking dance, leaping from one foot to the other and punching at the air with his fists.

Diana crumpled. She wanted to curl up and die. The fat man took another photograph.

'Leave me *alone*!' she pleaded. '*Please*!'

'*Yeah*! Leave her *alone*, why don't you?'

Diana turned. Someone had come up behind her: a girl dressed in black, about her own age. She was wearing a scuffed leather jacket. She looked tough. She looked like the sort of person who would normally make Diana a little nervous, but right now Diana had never been so glad to see someone in her life.

'Why don't you piss off,' the fat man said nastily. 'We're the press.'

'I don't give a shit who you are,' the girl said. 'You've got no right to treat her like dogmeat.' She took a step towards Paul. Peck tried to bundle her out of the way. Casually, with the air of someone who'd done it many times before, she brought her knee up into his groin.

The photographer made an 'Oof!' sound and doubled up in agony. His face went a slick greenish-grey colour.

'Jesus Christ!' the reporter exclaimed. He backed out of the way, eyeing the girl warily as she took another step towards him.

Diana pulled herself together. She grabbed the stranger's arm and marched her up to the front door. She came up with the right key first time. She bundled her rescuer into the hall and slammed the door shut behind them.

'Way to go!' the girl said. Diana realised for the first time that she had an American accent.

'Blasted muckrakers,' she said, trying with difficulty to insert another key into the door of her flat. Her hands were shaking now. She wanted to collapse into a chair.

She got the door open, and turned back. The girl in black was standing in the middle of the hallway, gazing up at the stairs with a peculiar expression on her face, as though she was trying to remember something. She was shivering.

'Please do come in,' Diana said. 'I owe you a drink, at least.'

The girl's head jerked round at the sound of Diana's voice. 'Sure,' she said. 'Thanks. I could do with one.' She went past Diana into the flat.

Diana remember her manners. They hadn't been introduced.

'I'm sorry,' she said. 'My name's Diana Markham. And I'm extremely grateful. You've just saved me from a fate worse than death at the hands of the gutter press.'

She held out her hand. The girl looked at it, suddenly unsure of herself, and then shook it tentatively. 'Hi, Diana. Pleased to meet you,' she said. 'I'm Jenny Hoffman.'

'Thank God you came along when you did,' Diana said. 'Those men won't leave me alone.'

Jenny walked slowly around the kitchen, taking in the unpacked crates, the almost-empty shelves and the gaps in the fittings. 'You've just moved in here, right?'

'That's right,' said Diana. 'The other flats are still empty.' She hovered in the doorway, uncertain of what to do next. 'There's champagne in the fridge. Will that do?'

'Sure,' said Jenny. She went over to the window. 'They're still out there, I think. I can see the top of some guy's head over the hedge. I can't see too well from here.'

41

'You'll have to lie low till the coast is clear. I hope you're not in a hurry.' Diana found herself giggling as she felt around in one of the crates and unwrapped a couple of wine glasses from wads of newspaper. 'Did you see his face when you walloped him?'

'Yeah, he looked like a stuck pig,' said Jenny. 'Gross. Serves the scumbag right. What have they got on you, anyway? You a celebrity or something?'

Diana wasn't quite sure how to reply. 'I don't know,' she said at last. 'I don't know *what* they want. I'm completely *ordinary*. It's just that . . . well, my father owns a few horses, things like that. He's sort of a distant relative of the Duke of Monmouth's descendants. That sort of thing.'

It sounded ridiculous once she'd said it. She hoped she didn't sound like a spoilt little rich girl. She hoped the American girl would understand. Americans weren't supposed to be as obsessed with class as the British.

Jenny whistled through her teeth. She sounded impressed. 'I get it,' she said. 'Definitely uptown.'

Diana could see her digesting the information, and was thankful when her manner didn't change abruptly, as so many people's did. She didn't become obsequious, nor did she get aggressive. In fact, Jenny didn't look as though she cared two hoots. She appeared to be more interested in her surroundings.

'What's through there?' she asked, inclining her head towards the lounge. 'Can I take a look?'

'Please do,' said Diana. 'There's not much to look at yet, but make yourself at home. I'll get the shampoo out. Veuve Cliquot or Canard-Duchêne?'

Jenny shrugged. 'Yeah, the French one.' She wandered out of the kitchen and into the next room.

The lounge smelt of new carpet. It almost looked lived in, but not quite: the furniture seemed to have been positioned for effect, rather than convenience. There was

42

an odd mixture of bric-à-brac on the shelf units by the filled-in fireplace: some tasteful glass ornaments, one or two empty vases, and a few items that looked drastically out of place. Jenny guessed that maybe they were family heirlooms. The clock was like something out of an old movie. Next to it was a bakelite radio with a shell-shaped dial. Definitely retro-tech, she decided. But maybe worth a bit.

There were also some books and records lying around, along with a few magazines. First steps towards personal clutter, Jenny thought. It was as though someone had made an effort to get the place looking comfortable, instead of like a perfectly ordered illustration from a housekeeping journal.

A battered old teddybear was propped up against the cushions on the sofa. Jenny picked it up, clutching it to her as she sauntered around the room. Every so often she paused to examine the framed photographs more closely or to read what was printed on the spines of the books. They were mostly well-thumbed classics: Lewis Carroll, some Dickens and Jane Austen, together with some titles Jenny didn't recognise. It looked as though Diana liked to read.

Without really thinking, she drew out her packet of cigarettes and lit one. Even as she drew on it, she realised she couldn't see an ashtray in the room. Oh-oh, she thought. It was a No Smoking Zone. Like Beverly Hills. Looking round guiltily, she stubbed the cigarette out on the sole of her boot and slid it back into the packet. She fanned her arms, trying to dispel the smoke.

She was still wafting the air when Diana came in with a bottle and two wine glasses. 'I see you've managed to get acquainted with Melrose,' she said.

'What? Oh yeah, the grizzly bear. It was love at first sight. I really dig these older guys, you know.' She flipped the teddy's one remaining ear. 'You really call him

Melrose? That's cute. There's a place in LA they must have named for him.'

Diana tore off the wire and applied her thumbs to the cork, which eased out with a hollow *thunk*. A wisp of gas curled up from the neck of the bottle. 'Melrose has been in our family for three generations,' she said proudly. 'He belonged to my grandmother and mother before me.'

Jenny sat herself down on the sofa and plonked Melrose down beside her. 'A family man, eh? Well, that's how I like 'em! Older and wiser!'

Diana laughed. She liked this American girl. Her appearance was a little odd, but she had rather a sweet face. When she wasn't beating up photographers, that is. Jenny looked as though she could take care of herself, and Diana admired that. She wished she'd been able to be as aggressive. It was no good trying to be reasonable with men like that.

The champagne fizzed as she poured it. She handed one of the glasses to Jenny. 'Sorry it's not a proper glass. They're still at the bottom of a crate somewhere, waiting to be unpacked.'

'No problem,' said Jenny, who couldn't see anything wrong with the wine glass she was holding. She stood up and clinked it against Diana's. 'Death to the scumbag muckrakers!'

'Absolutely!' said Diana. 'Cheers!'

They drank, both of them trying to think of something else to say. Jenny pointed to one of the photographs.

'Who's the military dude? Your father?'

'Dude? Oh no, no. That's Oliver. We're going to be married in two weeks' time.' She held out her hand so that Jenny could see the engagement ring.

'*Really?*' said Jenny. She looked from the photo to Diana's hand and back again. 'Well, congratulations. I hope you'll both be real happy together. Here's to you and the captain!' She raised her glass again.

Diana stared at her fiancé's photograph. Did he really look that old? It was probably just the uniform. And Oliver was looking very stern. Like a figure of authority, she thought, remembering what Deborah had said.

'So how long have you been here?' asked Jenny, leaning back and crossing her ankles. Diana found herself gazing at the American's boots, which had long, pointed toes and an array of metal buckles up the side.

'Oh, a couple of weeks,' she said. 'We're in the process of moving in, really. I'm just staying here for a while to try and get things sorted out.'

'Your boyfriend as well?'

'No, he's stuck at the airbase. He's taking a couple of weeks off for our honeymoon, so they're driving him extra hard in advance to make up for it. He's a test-pilot.'

'Who lived here before you?'

'I'm sorry, I've no idea,' said Diana. She was suddenly irritated by the questions. Jenny seemed to be asking an awful lot of them. 'Hey,' she said. 'You're not a reporter as well, are you?'

'No, no,' said Jenny. 'Sorry. I didn't meant to give you the third degree. Just curious, that's all.'

'Well I'm sorry, I don't know who lived here before us,' Diana said, a little stiffly. 'It was empty for a long time, I think. Daddy gave me the whole house as a wedding present.'

There was an awkward pause. Jenny looked taken aback. Diana felt like biting her tongue off. She wished she hadn't made that last remark. *Terrific*, she thought. How to make friends and influence people: just remind them of how much money you've got.

'Look,' she said. 'I'm sorry. Those reporters have put me on edge. I'm sorry, I hope I didn't sound as if . . .'

'No, not at all,' said Jenny. 'Why do you keep on saying sorry? You've got nothing to apologise for.'

Diana wondered whether there wasn't a hint of sarcasm

45

in her voice. She decided not. Jenny seemed too open and friendly for that.

'How about you?' she said, trying to change the subject. 'Where are you from?'

'LA,' said Jenny. 'That is . . . I . . . *Jesus!* This is too weird.'

'Weird?'

Jenny took a deep breath. 'I'm not really from LA. I mean, I've just come from there, but it's not where I'm *from*. I think I'm from here.'

'You mean your ancestors were British?'

'No, no. I mean right *here*. This house. I mean . . .' She trailed off helplessly. Diana felt a twinge of alarm.

'You mean you were coming here anyway? You weren't just walking past when you saw me with those reporters?'

'Don't get paranoid,' said Jenny. 'I wasn't coming to see *you*. I was coming to see the *house*. I thought if I came here I could maybe pick up some vibes or something.'

'Vibes,' echoed Diana. 'I'm afraid I don't understand.'

Warning bells were sounding in her brain, Jenny had been acting oddly ever since they had come in. Diana had put it down to her being American, a stranger in a strange land, but now she wasn't so sure. She was grateful for Jenny's help outside, there was no question about that. But now she wished she hadn't been quite so quick off the mark inviting her in for a drink. It wasn't the sort of thing she normally did. She didn't normally talk to strangers.

'I guess you think I'm a weirdo, right?' asked Jenny. Diana didn't reply. It was exactly what she had been thinking. 'Well, I'll admit it sounds weird,' Jenny went on. 'I mean, it even sounds weird to *me*. I don't know who my parents are, you see. I don't even know what they looked like.'

'You're an orphan?' Diana felt a sudden rush of guilt. 'I'm sorry, I didn't know . . .'

Jenny laughed. 'An orphan? I guess so, though that makes me sound like Little Orphan Annie or something. It's not that. I never *felt* like an orphan. I mean, I grew up with these guys thinking they were my parents. And then out of nowhere I got this letter from a solicitor telling me that my aunt had died. I didn't even know I *had* an aunt. But she left me some money, whoever she was – it wasn't so much money but it was okay, pretty good. And then it all started to come out. It turned out that Ernest and Mae weren't my mom and dad after all. They'd adopted me when I was six years old.'

'So you decided to find out who your real parents were?' Diana was intrigued now. She had sometimes fantasised about being an orphan. The heroines in stories and comic-books had always been orphans.

'Yeah, that's about it,' Jenny said. She paused. 'Except . . . Well, there's a whole load of missing pieces. Nobody will tell me anything. I guess they don't really know too much themselves. And I . . . *I don't remember anything.*'

'You were very young,' Diana said sympathetically.

'But I don't remember a *thing*,' said Jenny. 'Zilch. I mean, *nada*. That's kind of weird, isn't it? It's all a blank, all of my life up until Ernest and Mae.'

'They sound like nice people,' said Diana, not knowing what else to say.

'Oh, I don't know,' said Jenny. 'They were like any other parents, I guess. We didn't get on too well at times, but they were okay. They were just regular parents. They behaved like parents, Jesus, I even *looked* like them.' She rubbed her nose. 'I reckon they were more upset than I was when I got the letter.'

Diana topped up their glasses with more champagne. 'Have you any idea who your real parents were?'

'Not really. All I know is they were English. And they used to live in this house.'

'That's easy, then,' said Diana. 'We just find out where they moved to.'

'No,' said Jenny. 'This was their last address. They . . . died here.'

Diana felt as though she had put her foot in it. 'Oh, Jenny, I'm so sorry.'

The American girl seemed to have shrunk, all pep drained from her. She sat slumped on the sofa, gazing into her glass.

Diana wanted desperately to cheer her up. 'Never mind,' she said, putting an arm round Jenny's shoulders. 'We can find out their names from the estate agent or something.'

'Yeah,' said Jenny. 'That's about it.'

'Where are you staying? Have you got a hotel?'

Jenny nodded.

'Tell you what,' Diana said. 'Why don't you come round here tomorrow? There's a lot of old junk down in the basement. It could have been there for years. You never know, there might be something there you recognise. We can go through it together, if you like.'

Jenny perked up slightly. 'Oh yeah? That might be interesting. You don't mind me poking around?'

'Don't be silly. Of course not. We'll have to clear out that stuff sooner or later anyway. And it'll be good to have company while Ollie's away.'

'You mean it? That'd be great, Diana. Thanks.' Jenny drained her glass and got to her feet. 'I'd better be going. Hey, you don't suppose those guys are still out there, do you?'

Diana craned her head to look through the window. The street, as far as she could see, was empty. 'I can't see them. They must have got bored.'

'Yeah,' said Jenny. 'Hey, your phone's working, isn't it? Give me a ring tomorrow, right?' She rooted around in her pocket for a book of matches from the hotel. 'That's the number. Don't forget, it's Hoffman, Jenny Hoffman, Room 424. And look, call the cops if those scumbags start bothering you again. Better still, call *me*. I'd be happy to kick them in the nuts for you.'

'All right,' said Diana, taking the matchbook. 'Thanks. I'll remember that.' She felt purposeful and efficient again. Listening to Jenny's problems had taken her mind off her own. After all, she reasoned, getting married was only a minor trauma. At least she knew who she was. It wasn't likely that she'd ever be allowed to forget it, either.

'You'll be okay?' Jenny asked as she left. 'Don't forget: if they give you any shit, just pick up the phone and yell.'

'I will do,' Diana promised. She felt more confident now. She felt she could easily deal with Paul Lawrence and Peck if they gave her any trouble. 'See you tomorrow, then.'

It was only after her guest had gone that Diana remembered the doll. She had stuffed it into a polythene bag and buried it in one of the crates. It seemed too valuable to throw out, and the head could probably be repaired. But she wasn't too keen on having it lying around, not after the nightmare.

Now she wondered if it had been one of Jenny's old toys. She hoped not.

Still feeling efficient, Diana unpacked one of the crates and stowed its contents in a kitchen cupboard. The day hadn't been wasted entirely; she had managed to get *something* done, at least. She would see to the rest in the morning. She felt too tired now to do anything else.

She settled back on the sofa to watch television. At last she felt in control of things. More or less. She thought about the house. There had been deaths here. Jenny had said that her parents had died here. Diana found herself wondering how they'd died. She hoped there hadn't been anything too unpleasant about it.

She hoped too that, whatever had happened, it hadn't happened in the room where she was now sitting. But if it had, then it wouldn't necessarily mean that the place was haunted, would it? That was too silly; there were no such things as ghosts. But could a room remain completely normal after someone had died there? Perhaps the room recorded their last moments and replayed them again and again, like a video machine. And occasionally, just occasionally, someone who was on the same wavelength might come along, and then they'd see something.

Stop it. Diana told herself sternly. Stop thinking morbid thoughts. Concentrate on the television programme.

There was a talking head on the screen. Diana recognised it as a junior MP who was trying to squeeze a controversial bill through parliament. She decided she must have met him at some point. Or perhaps she had seen him on television before. His argument, or what she could grasp of it, did sound tremendously familiar. He was haranguing an unseen audience about the sanctity of . . . what? Life? Marriage? the National Health Service? Possibly all three.

'There is a normality and decency that is absolute,' he was saying. 'And we take that, and twist it into untold obscene variations. People become confused. There are so many choices, each presenting itself as though it were a viable alternative, when in fact it is corrupt, monstrous, a hideous travesty of real life . . .'

Diana yawned and switched channels, but there was nothing of interest on any of them. In fact, the MP seemed to be on all four channels at once. She pointed the remote control at the set to switch it off. Lord, she thought, how she hated party political broadcasts! She picked up a copy of *Harpers & Queen* and began to flick through it. Then flung it down in annoyance. She'd seen that issue before. The faces were all familiar.

*   *   *

Peck stood in front of the house, looking up at it. The upper windows were empty. There didn't seem to be anyone living there. The only lights were on the ground floor.

So that was where she was.

He'd seen the American tart leave. He'd been tempted to follow her down the road and give her a whack round the head, but his professional instincts had got the better of him. Besides, she'd been a bit too nifty with the knee. He'd puked his noodles up all over Paulie's car, and Paulie had been pretty miffed. Miffed enough to leave him stranded here on his own. But Peck didn't mind. He fancied hanging around for a bit.

Anyway, it looked like the American tart had got well in with Miss Fancy Pants. Probably sniffed the money. Americans could smell it a mile off. She'd be back, he was sure of that. And he'd get even with her.

But that would have to wait.

Now, Peck thought, there was work to be done. He chortled, patting his Nikon affectionately. He loved his work. His work was *fun*.

He decided to check out the back of the house. There was a small fence to negotiate. He ripped the sleeve of his jacket getting over it, but it didn't matter; the jacket was on its way out anyway. There were stains all down the front, and splashes of vomit. Peck didn't worry too much about his clothes, but he drew the line at going round coated in yesterday's regurgitated lunch.

The windows at the back were dark. Peck tried to peer through. It looked as if one of the rooms was a bedroom, but he couldn't see much. He trampled through some shrubbery and found the back door. It was locked. He swore. He thought about smashing the glass, but it was reinforced. Probably be more trouble than it was worth. He went round to the front again.

The light was still on at the front. The curtains were drawn, so he couldn't see anything, but he knew she was in there. Smarmy stuck-up bitch. He'd show her. She wouldn't be so smarmy and stuck-up when she saw her photo on the front page. And he'd make sure it was a good one.

*   *   *

The sound of the telephone jerked her awake. She had dozed off without realising. The magazine lay on the floor where she'd dropped it. She reached out and picked up the receiver.

'Hello? . . . Hello? Ollie!'

There was no answer. There was no sound at all, not even breathing. Then she thought she heard a distant voice.

'Hello,' said the voice, 'we're putting you through. Go ahead.'

There was a click, followed by the purr of the dialling tone. Diana checked her watch, Oliver usually called at about this time. Perhaps he was having trouble with the connection. She picked up her handbag and hunted through for her address book. Then she pushed the number for the airbase.

The phone rang for a long time, perhaps two or three minutes. Then someone picked it up. A man's voice answered, a little diffidently, as though she'd interrupted something important.

'I'd like to speak to Flight Lieutenant Hall, please,' Diana said.

'Hold the line,' said the voice at the other end. She waited for what seemed like an age. There was a dead silence at the other end. Just when she was beginning to wonder if they'd been cut off, the man's voice came back on. 'He's off for this week. Can anyone else help?'

'That's impossible,' Diana said. 'You must be mistaken. I know he's there.'

'Sorry,' said the voice. 'No mistake. Would you like to leave a message?'

'Yes, could you tell him that Diana Markham called. His fiancée. Please ask him to ring me. It's important.'

'Will do,' said the voice, a little too promptly. Diana had the feeling that her message hadn't been written down and would be forgotten within seconds. The man on the line, whoever he was, didn't exactly sound as though he were bursting to help.

She hung up, surprised and confused. Oliver had told her he'd be at the base. It was unlike him to change his plans like that; he would have let her know. He was probably there after all, she decided. There must have been a mix-up. The man must have made a mistake.

She checked her watch again. It was a quarter to twelve. Time for bed. She felt quite confident of sleeping soundly tonight. Talking to Deborah had been a help, and so had the meeting with Jenny. And so, she was forced to admit, had the champagne.

She padded around getting ready for bed. How wonderful, she thought, to have a bathroom that was for her use and for her use only. No caps left off the toothpaste tube, no damp towels left steaming on the floor. She supposed that Oliver would be bringing in razors and cans of shaving foam and whatever else it was that men used in bathrooms. But, for now, it was hers. All hers.

She went back into the bedroom and slipped out of her skirt and blouse, folding them neatly over the back of a chair. The window opened out onto the gardens at the back of the house. She hadn't bothered to draw the curtains; there didn't seem to be much point. Outside, there was a narrow terrace which she planned to fill with tubs and troughs. Beyond that, trees and bushes blocked the view of the buildings across the way.

Formless patches of light were just visible through the foliage.

She was standing in her underwear when a dog began to bark outside. It sounded very close. Just outside the window, in fact. There was a faint rustling from the bushes. She got up and pulled the curtains across. She had never lived on the ground floor before. The rules were different here. She had to remember that people could see in. Peeping Toms, perhaps. She had to remember to keep the curtains drawn.

It was while she was pulling her nightdress over her head that she heard the floorboard creak in the next room. There was no reason to panic. There was nothing to get spooked about. It was an old building, and old buildings were full of peculiar noises. Her parents' house was exactly the same.

But, just to reassure herself, she slipped her dressing-gown on and stuck her head round the door. Of course there was no one there.

And then she felt her heart skip a beat. The door to the flat was open. Just a crack. But it was definitely open.

She'd locked it. She was sure she had. She remembered saying goodbye to Jenny, and . . . Had she *really* forgotten to close the door? Oh Lord, she thought. She hadn't drunk *that* much champagne.

She walked forward to close the door. Cool air ruffled her hair as she reached it. A night breeze was blowing through the hallway outside. Orange shadows shifted on the floor in the semi-darkness.

She saw to her horror that the front door was also open.

Diana could have kicked herself. What was the point of having expensive locks fitted if she was going to forget to use them? It was like an open invitation to anyone who passed by, she thought grimly. She padded out of her flat and pushed the front door shut.

And as the latch clicked precisely into place, she heard a noise behind her. A door banging.

She knew what it was even before she had turned back. Please God, she thought, let it not be the door to her flat. Let it be anything but that.

She turned. The door to her flat had slammed itself shut. She was locked out.

Diana groaned. She felt like tearing her hair out. She was in her night clothes, barefoot, without keys or money. Oliver had keys, but Oliver wasn't here. She was locked out. Damn and blast.

She pressed the light switch. Nothing happened. The bulb had gone. The hallway remained in shadow. *Oh God*, she thought, *what now?*

Out of the darkness by the staircase there came a soft, throaty chuckle. Diana felt herself go weak at the knees. She was not alone. There was someone else in the hallway.

Slowly, as though deliberately stringing out the suspense, the bulky figure of a man emerged from the shadows by the stairs. He was made even bulkier by the objects hanging from his neck: a large black battery pack and a camera with a flashgun attached. She recognised him with a sinking feeling. It was Peck.

He chuckled again as he approached. It was not a nice sound. Oh God, Diana thought wearily. He'd got her cornered. It was the last straw. This, she could have done without.

It was cool in the hallway, but Peck was sweating. She could see his face shining in the half-light. His flesh was puffy and grey; he looked even more disgusting than she remembered. His breathing was hoarse, almost wheezing. The thought of him coming any closer was more than she could bear. She backed away from him into the crook of the passageway. If only the door to her flat were open. But it wasn't. She was trapped.

'Get out,' she said, trying to sound angry instead of frightened. 'You're not supposed to be here.'

He stopped a few feet in front of her. He was playing with something, teasing her. Tossing it in the air, catching it again in a podgy hand. Deftly. Once, perhaps, he had been good at ballgames. A long time ago.

Whatever the object was, it was very small. And it glittered as it span through the faint orange light.

'Hiya,' he said. He didn't have to say anything more. He smiled at her, and she felt her knees, already weak, turn to jelly. The smile said that he knew they were alone together. It said that he could see she wasn't properly dressed. And it said that he knew who she was. And that he didn't care. To him, she was nothing but dogmeat. All the money in the world wouldn't help her now.

'Get out!' said Diana. 'Get out before I call the police!'

Peck's eyebrows shot up. He peered around in exaggerated surprise. 'Ooooh,' he said, 'is there a phone out here? Perhaps I could call my editor, in that case. Got a story. I *mean*, "Scantily-clad Society Girl Locked Out of Love Nest". Hot Stuff.' The mocking expression gave way to another leer. 'Come on, sweetie. Let's not kid around.'

He took a step forward. Diana looked around for something to defend herself with. There was nothing. The hallway was completely bare. She was on her own. She had nothing but her wits, and, as far as she could make out, they weren't working too well. Only a complete idiot would have let herself get caught like this.

'It's just you and me, darling,' he said, sidling closer. 'You've got something I want. And I've got something *you* want. Maybe we can do a trade.' He grinned, bunching his fist in front of her face and unpeeling the fingers to reveal what was secreted in his sweaty palm.

It was a ring.

It was like her own engagement ring, Diana saw, only

smaller, dwarfed by the fleshy mounts of the fat man's hand. She raised her own hand. Just to check.

Her finger was bare. The engagement ring had gone.

The truth crept up on her with mind-numbing slowness. She didn't know how, but the fat man had her ring. *He had her ring.* He was taunting her with it. He was holding it up between thumb and forefinger. Moistening the little finger on his other hand with the tip of his tongue. Pushing it in and out through the hole. Chuckling.

'How did you get that?' she cried. 'Give it back!' She made to grab the ring, but Peck swiped it out of her reach.

'Naughty, naughty,' he said, waggling his finger at her. 'If girly-wurly wants her gew-gaw, she's gonna have to be a whole lot nicer to Uncle Pecky-wecky.'

'Give it to me,' Diana hissed through gritted teeth. She felt like killing him.

Peck made a piglike noise through his nose. 'Oh, so you want it, do you?' he said. 'Miss High and Mighty wants it, does she? Well, then . . . Perhaps we ought to *give* it to her.'

She had no idea that anyone so fat could move so swiftly. One moment he was rocking on his heels, gazing at her through puffy eyelids. The next instant, he was lunging at her.

It was time to scream. She opened her mouth. But it was too late. She was enveloped in folds of flesh and the sound was smothered before it reached the air. The man was like a sumo wrestler. She stood no chance against him.

She tried to bring her knee up into his groin, as Jenny had done earlier, but there was no room to move. Something fat and squidgy was clamped over her open mouth. She bit down on it as hard as she could.

Peck squealed. The folds of flesh dropped away, just enough to let her squirm out of his grasp. She slipped away from him and made a dash for the back door.

She felt a grim sense of irony as she struggled in vain to open it. The back door, at least, she had remembered to lock. And she didn't have the key. She tugged at the knob, but the door refused to open.

'Coooeee!' Peck was coming for her.

If only she'd gone in the other direction. She could have made it through the front door and onto the street. But it was too late now. She was cornered. She couldn't see him, but she knew he was there, waiting by the stairs. She flattened herself against the wall.

She had forgotten the door to the basement. The door-knob prodded into her spine, reminding her. She opened the door and went in, pulling it shut behind her.

It was dark in there. Darker than the hallway. She reached for the light switch. She touched something cold and wet. She snatched her hand back with a surprised yelp. She could just see her fingers in the dead light that was filtering through the grimy window. They were covered in slime. The walls were coated with it.

It had been damp when she'd come down here before. But not this damp. There'd been no rain, so where was the moisture coming from? It was running down the walls. No, not running. It was oozing, dripping. She could hear the steady *spat-spat-spat* of a tap or a leaking pipe, somewhere down there in the dark. It reminded her of something, but she couldn't think what. She didn't want to go down there. She didn't want to go down there at all.

But she had no choice. It was her only chance. Peck wouldn't be able to find her in the darkness. She could hide, she could hide for ever, and he'd get bored and go away. She started to grope her way down the steps, managing to suppress the nausea that rose up in her throat at the feel of the slimy walls.

There were more stairs than she remembered. They

seemed to go on and on. Her feet were numb with cold, but she went down and down, testing each step as she descended. She didn't want to fall. She didn't want to lay there like her grandfather, helpless, in the dark and cold. Especially with Peck coming after her.

After what seemed like hours, she found herself on level ground. She stumbled towards the corner where she remembered seeing the pile of mouldy carpeting, the broken bedstead. She missed it in the dark. Her toes stubbed against something hard, and then there was nothing. She was clutching at emptiness.

The emptiness went on and on.

There was a mechanical whirr and a blinding flash of lightning from somewhere above her. A voice cried 'Helloooo!', like a hunting call. She was left staggering, blinking red in the dark. But, in the instant of the flash, the basement had come up bright and sharp like a snapshot. And it wasn't like she remembered it at all. She'd got it all wrong. She was standing at a junction. Passageways stretched in all directions, fading into infinity.

She wondered vaguely how she'd managed to blunder past the boiler and the piles of broken furniture. This was a part of the basement she hadn't been in before. Either that, or she'd lost her sense of visual perspective. It was no use now looking for a heap of junk to hide behind. There was no junk here at all.

The flash went off again. She caught a brief glimpse of Peck, standing at the top of the basement steps. He was miles away. She had a head start on him. But he began to descend, firing off flashes as he came. Heedless of the darkness now, she turned to run into its embrace. Anything to get away from the advancing lens and the fat man oozing flesh behind it. She ran, and her feet splashed through a shallow pool of water.

'How about a nice wet T-shirt shot?' Peck called from somewhere behind her. He sounded as though he was choking on his own laughter. He was finding the whole situation hilarious.

Diana kept going. Was there no end to the basement? In the next flash, she had a brief vision of a low, vaulted ceiling fashioned from crumbling brick. The passageway narrowed.

She forced herself to go on. Down the passageway, and a twist to the right. This was madness, she realised. This couldn't be happening. There was a distant rumbling somewhere to her left. It sounded like some monstrous machinery, wheels turning and cables straining under a great weight. But now she could see nothing at all: only the darkness as she pressed on, eyes straining to catch a glimpse of something. There had to be a way out. There had to be.

She had somehow found her way into a vast subterranean labyrinth. And there was no thread to lead her to safety.

Now she knew what this place reminded her of. Many years ago, when she was eight or nine, she'd gone with her family to see friends in Somerset. They'd visited caves dripping with lime. The paths had been quite safe; they'd been marked out with railings and floodlights. But at one stage the guide had gathered his party around him and flicked a switch. The darkness had been total. The silence had been broken only by a few nervous giggles and a distant dripping sound. The caves went on for ever, the guide had said. Anyone foolish enough to stray from the pathway might never be seen or heard of again.

There were no stalactites here. These weren't natural caves. They were man-made, but they felt as though nothing human had passed that way for years. Diana wondered if she would ever be able to find her way back.

But then her eyes picked out the glint of metal. It looked like a reflective sign, set into the wall. She could just about make out what it said: *Danger*.

The reflection was being cast by a greenish glow. It came from somewhere up ahead. She edged forward cautiously, keeping one hand on the wall. The roof was as high as a cathedral. Diana tipped her face back to stare at the strange rock formations overhead; they didn't look man-made, but some of them were shaped roughly like human figures clinging to the rocky vaults, as though people had been caught and turned to stone while trying to climb their way out.

She was so fascinated by the rock formations that she almost forgot to look where she was going. Her knee crashed against something hard and cold. She'd walked into the top of a metal ladder, fixed by bolts embedded in the rock. She'd been lucky; it was the first bit of luck she'd had all evening. If she hadn't walked into the ladder . . .

Diana shuddered to think what might have happened. She peered down. The ground came to an abrupt end. Beyond that, there was nothing: a sheer drop into a pit. She couldn't see the bottom, but the greenish glow came from somewhere down there, giving the whole cavern an eerie cast. The glow was shifting slowly, as though reflected off water; an underground stream, perhaps, winding through the bowels of the earth.

There was a wheezing and a snuffling behind her. She heard Peck's footsteps, ricocheting off the walls of the passageway.

She was caught between the Devil and the Deep Green Sea. She paused, but not for long. There was only one way to go, as far as she could see. And if that way led further down, well, she'd worry about finding her way to the surface later. She had to get away from the fat man.

Without giving herself time to reconsider, she took hold of the top of the ladder and swung her legs down, feeling for the rungs with her feet. The metal creaked, one of the plates straining under her weight to work its way loose of the rock. She clung to the topmost rung, praying that the bolts would hold, praying that she wouldn't lose her grip.

She lowered her foot. It trod on the empty air. She looked down and wished she hadn't. There was no next step. The ladder was shorn off after only seven rungs. Below that, there was nothing. Only the waiting pit.

She looked up again and a flash caught her full in the face. When the dancing dots had cleared, she saw Peck's enormous head grinning down at her. He raised the viewfinder to his eye, preparing to press the shutter again

'Hold it!' he exclaimed. 'Don't move. That's beautiful! Just . . . lick your lips a little, will you!' The flash went off again.

Diana twisted sideways on the ladder, trying to get out of the firing line. She opened her mouth to plead with him, but the only sound that emerged was a whimper.

'Hmm,' said Peck, looking at her thoughtfully. 'We could do with a bit of Neo-Realism here.' He adjusted his stance. His foot came down heavily on the top rung of the ladder, trapping Diana's hand between his boot and the metal. She screamed as fierce pain shot up her arm. He ground her knuckles beneath his massive weight.

'Still want your ring back?' he asked nastily. 'You just have to ask, you know.' He sank down onto his haunches and dangled the ring in front of her. Had she been on firm ground, she could have grabbed it easily. But it was all she could do to hang onto the ladder

'You . . . bastard . . .' she gasped. 'I hope you rot in hell . . .' With her free hand she struggled to pull herself back up, but it was no good. Peck leered down at her.

She wasn't sure what happened next. It was all too quick. But the light changed. The green of the cavern was suddenly diffused by a flickering, orange glow. Peck saw it too. She saw him look up, startled.

There was an unearthly sound; a high-pitched shrieking like that of an animal in pain. No human being could have made a sound like that. It was getting louder.

It came from the passageway behind Peck. Diana saw his head turn, an expression of shock and disbelief passing quickly across his face.

'Hang on . . .' he protested. 'We didn't . . .'

His voice was drowned out by the shrieking as something came flying out of the passageway behind him. The flashgun fired, and then there was a roaring and a wave of blistering heat. Peck was caught off balance. Something, it looked like a huge blazing torch except that it had arms and legs, swept past him and was gone, leaving the air shot with sparks dancing like fireflies.

Diana saw her ring spinning through the sparks, turning in a wide arc, over and down. One last gleam, and it had vanished into the pit.

And then it was Peck's turn. A more agile man might have been able to throw himself backwards. But the weight of the equipment slung round his neck pulled him down. The flash locked on automatic, or perhaps Peck's finger had frozen on the shutter release. There was a succession of dazzling strobe-like flashes which etched the images in Diana's brain; Peck flying over her head like a man shot from a cannon; Peck turning in a wild somersault with his fat arms flailing; Peck clutching at the empty air with his mouth open; Peck's body, smaller now, outlined against the waiting green glow.

His scream echoed from the walls as he tumbled down into the green-tinged darkness. Long after the flashes had stopped and she had lost sight of his body, the scream went on. Then it was cut off – suddenly.

Diana hung there for a moment, unable to believe what she had seen. Then, with a massive effort, she pulled herself up the ladder, shaking so badly that she could barely keep her grip. She hauled herself onto firm ground and collapsed, nursing her injured hand. The knuckles were torn and bleeding. She lay there unmoving for a while, unable to get up.

She couldn't feel sorry for Peck, but she remembered the look on his face as he had fallen, and she didn't feel glad. It was a horrible way for anyone to die. She hadn't meant him to die. She felt incredibly guilty, as though she had somehow caused him to fall. But it hadn't been her fault. Someone had pushed him, but it hadn't been her.

She had a sudden terrible thought that perhaps he wasn't dead after all. It was another one of his sick jokes. At any moment, his moonlike face would rise up over the edge of the pit. He would start taking photos again. She couldn't bring herself to look back down into the greenish glow. She didn't know what she might see. Perhaps a fat figure, struggling to pull itself up the rockface.

No, he was dead. He *had* to be dead. No one could have survived a fall like that.

She struggled wearily to her feet. The blackness of the tunnel beckoned, and she launched herself into it. There had to be a way out. She had found her way here, hadn't she? Then she would find her way out again. The passageway twisted and turned, and she followed it numbly. The darkness closed in around her. The darkness went on for ever. She gave herself up to it.

* * *

Diana opened her eyes. Light was coming through the curtains. Birds were chirping outside the window. She was in bed.

She was curled into a tight ball, and her feet were cold. The quilt had slipped and was hanging off the bed. She leaned out to pull it back around her. As she did so she caught sight of the sapphire on her finger.

'Oh Lord,' she said out loud. It had all been a dream.

64

The fat man, the basement, the bottomless pit; none of it had happened. She was in bed, and the ring was on her finger. She hugged herself with relief, snuggled down into the bed, and turned over onto her side.

And froze. She wasn't alone. There was a large body-sized lump under the quilt next to her. There was someone in bed with her. She could just see the top of someone's head. The hair was black and spiky, tinged with blue. She brought her hand up to touch it.

The hair moved. It wrapped itself around her fingers. She tugged, and it came away in her hand. She stared uselessly at the severed tangle of blue-black strands. There was a massive rocking motion as the body on the bed rolled over to meet her. Peck chuckled wetly as his pale face came to rest inches away from hers. The fat had eaten into his features. His breath smelt of soya sauce, and something else. His weight made an enormous dent in the mattress. Diana felt herself sliding down towards him. She scrabbled for the edge of the bed, but he pulled her back.

'Surprise!' he gurgled. 'You didn't think you'd get away from me that easily, did you?' His arms came up to enfold her in their clammy embrace.

'No!' she said, closing her eyes. 'This can't be happening.'

'You don't have to act ladylike with me,' he giggled. 'Not after last night.' The mattress heaved.

She recoiled as she felt a wet mouth tickling against her ear. He whispered something to her as she lost consciousness. She couldn't be sure, because the roaring in her head was too loud, but it sounded like: 'Two-way traffic now . . .'

THURSDAY

Diana opened her eyes. Light was coming through the curtains, and her feet were freezing. But she was on her own. There was no one in bed with her. She groaned in relief. Of *course* there was no one in bed with her. How *could* there have been?

'God, God, *God*,' she said out loud, pinching herself as hard as she could. This was real.

She started to tug the quilt up around her, and stopped, catching sight of her hand. It was aching, small twinges of dull pain. Her knuckles were scraped and bloodied. And her ring finger was bare. She stared at it for a full minute. Then she dived into action. She burrowed beneath the bedclothes, the pillow, feeling around frantically. There was nothing there. She rolled out of bed, landing on all fours to look beneath it.

There was nothing under the bed. 'Oh Lord,' she wailed. 'How could I have lost it?' Nothing on the bedside table, nothing on the dressing table, nothing on the floor. She whirled round in the middle of the room, trying desperately to remember where she'd left the ring. But she couldn't even remember taking it off.

There was a fumbling noise from the front door of the flat. She tensed up, nerves straining, wanting to scream. Someone was trying to get in.

She snatched up her dressing-gown, thrusting her arms into it as she raced to the front door. The fumbling noise continued. She hunkered down, eyeing the bolts, ready to pounce on them and slide them across. There was the noise of a key sliding into the lock. The door opened.

It wasn't Peck. How could it have been Peck? She felt a little ashamed of herself. Peck didn't have keys. Only Oliver had keys.

He was out of uniform, dressed in jeans and sweater. He looked at her, a little surprised to see his fiancée crouched catlike behind the door. He was clutching a small bunch of purple anemones. He held them out to her, rather shyly, saying 'How's my girl?'

Diana collapsed into his arms. 'Oliver, thank goodness it's you. I was having the most awful nightmare.' She felt rather foolish now.

'Well, nothing to worry about,' he said. 'I'm here now.'

He kissed her on the forehead. They went into the kitchen. Oliver put the flowers on the table, sat down and drew Diana onto his knee. He kissed her again.

'I must look a mess,' she said, breaking free of his arms. 'I don't think you should be allowed to see me in my nightie until after we're married. Just give me time to have a shower and get dressed and I'll fix us some breakfast.'

'Okay,' he said. 'That sounds great. But you'll have to lock the bathroom door. It's difficult enough as it is, keeping my hands off you, but the thought of you underneath that shower, soaping your naked body . . .'

'Oh, *Oliver*!' Diana blushed, and got to her feet. 'I won't be long,' she said.

'Okay,' said Oliver. 'I'll put the kettle on.' He began to say something else, but stopped, frowning. 'Where's your ring? My God, darling, what have you done to your hand?'

'Oh, I . . .' Diana looked down at her bloodied knuckles. She grabbed at the first excuse she could think of. 'I caught it against one of the crates. My finger was starting to swell. I took the ring off.'

She hated lying, but she particularly hated lying to Oliver. It was important for couples to tell the truth. It was important for them to trust each other. But she couldn't tell him what had happened to the ring until she found out what had happened for herself. It *had* to be somewhere.

Oliver took her injured hand and kissed it gently. 'Poor baby. Make sure you put some TCP on it, won't you.' She nodded, feeling guilty.

'I've got the stereo in the car,' he added. 'We can fix that up for you later on. I don't have to get back to the base until late afternoon.'

He was so sweet, Diana thought as she walked into the bathroom. She turned on the shower. She leant over the washbasin while the water heated up, staring at herself in the mirror. She looked terrible. She looked like *Margaret Thatcher*. She pulled a face. She wished she'd had time to clean herself up. She didn't like him seeing her like this.

But then, she supposed, he'd be seeing her like this every morning once they were married. He'd have to get used to it.

*   *   *

Later, when they'd had breakfast, she told him about the nightmares. She didn't go into too much detail, especially when it involved Oliver knocking her around, but he looked a little shocked whe she described how he'd lost his temper with her.

'Poor darling,' he said. 'You should have told me before. These wedding nerves are getting to you, aren't they? You don't *really* think of me as some kind of monster, do you?'

'Of course not!' Diana said.

'It sounds as though the press have been giving you a

68

hard time. You mustn't worry about them, you know. They're just doing their job.'

'That's exactly what *they* said.'

'Look, I'll phone the paper if you like. Ask them to leave you alone.'

'Oh, would you? I'd feel happier if you did.'

'Then it shall be done,' he said. He kissed her again.

'Things don't happen because you dream them, do they?'

Oliver laughed. 'Of course not. You're under strain, that's all. You did look a bit like a scared bunny rabbit when I arrived this morning, you know. I should have phoned, I suppose, but I thought you'd still be asleep. I didn't want to wake you.'

Diana made some more tea while he fetched some boxes from the car. He came back into the kitchen, hunting for something.

'Have you got a screwdriver, darling?'

'Oh, somewhere in that box, I think,' she said.

Oliver had a look.

'What's this?' he asked, pulling a bag out of the crate. He unwrapped the porcelain doll.

'Oh, that,' said Diana. 'I found it in the basement.'

She wasn't at all pleased to see the doll. She wished now that she'd put it in the dustbin.

'It looks as though it might be quite valuable,' Oliver said. 'You should get it mended.' He took it into the lounge with him.

They settled down and talked about arrangements and invitations and tickets. Oliver jotted down some phone numbers and promised to call Diana's parents.

'Oh, I'd like to invite Jenny to the wedding,' Diana said suddenly.

'Jenny?'

'You remember. The American girl I told you about.'

'If you like. That's fine by me.'

69

'Only she doesn't seem to know anyone in London. You'll like her. She's a bit odd, but sweet.' Diana searched through her handbag until she found the matchbook Jenny had given her. 'I'll give her a ring now,' she said. 'I told her she could come round this afternoon and look through some of the junk in the basement.'

* * *

The morning flew by. Diana pottered around happily, glad to have Oliver there. They went out to a small wine bar in the High Street to have lunch. Diana felt slightly tipsy after two glasses of white wine. Oliver made her laugh with his impersonations of the officers at the base. He told her about the glitches on the new chunk of hardware he was testing; it was supposed to be Top Secret, but Diana couldn't have repeated any of it to anyone, even if she'd wanted to. It all sounded immensely complicated and technical.

As soon as they got back to the flat, Oliver started to tackle the stereo system. She watched him for a while, but soon got bored. She would have been content with something less sophisticated, but Oliver enjoyed tinkering with machines and she knew it. An ordinary shop-bought stereo wasn't enough for him; he had to take everything to pieces and reassemble it. Diana wasn't sure that she would be able to hear the difference, but she took his word for it that his customised version would be a vast improvement.

He was fiddling with the speakers when the doorbell went. It was Jenny. Diana pressed the entryphone button and let her in.

Diana had never even considered the possibility that Oliver and Jenny might not get on. She was surprised, and a little upset, by the frosty manner in which Oliver greeted the American girl. Jenny, for her part, remained aloof on the other side of the room. Diana tried in vain to draw her into the conversation.

Oliver was a little suspicious. He'd met most of Diana's friends. He was used to seeing them kitted out in designer wear, or Burberry and Aquascutum. He'd expected the American girl to be the Beverly Hills equivalent, but she looked as though she'd done her shopping at Oxfam. And her *hair*; it was dreadful. Oliver thought she looked like a cheap punk.

Jenny, when she'd been introduced, thought she had glimpsed an expression on Oliver's face which was a distant cousin to the desk clerk's sneer. She felt like saying something snappy, but then the expression was gone and he'd been all smiles and politeness. Maybe she was getting paranoid about her appearance. It didn't really fit in here, she knew.

Besides, if Diana was marrying this dude, then he had to have his good points. She couldn't actually *see* any, but they had to be there. Okay, he was good-looking, so long as you went for guys who looked like Barbie's boyfriend Ken. But Christ, he was a cold fish.

Watch it, Hoffman, she told herself. *Keep that lip buttoned.* Her mouth had got her into enough trouble in the past. And she liked Diana. Diana was a good sort. She didn't want to upset her.

Besides, she *really* wanted to take a look in that basement.

'She's a peculiar girl,' Oliver said when Jenny had gone into the kitchen to make coffee. 'She doesn't seem your type at all.'

'Oh, she's terribly nice,' Diana said, feeling it was important that Oliver should like Jenny. 'She's had a lot of bad luck.' She had already told him about Jenny's search for her parents, but now she told him again, in greater detail. He was sliding small pieces of cardboard beneath the stereo deck, checking the surface with a spirit

71

level. He didn't seem terribly interested in what Diana was saying, though he looked at her strangely, she thought, when she mentioned that Jenny had lived in their house a long time ago.

'I had no idea,' he said. 'I had no idea the house was so important. There must be a key.'

'Yes,' Diana said, though she wasn't sure what he was talking about. It was unlike Oliver to be so vague. 'There must be a key to Jenny's past here,' she agreed. Later, when she thought about it, she wondered whether perhaps he hadn't said '*She* must be a key.' But that would have made even less sense.

He stood up, finally, twiddling the knobs. The face of the stereo lit up with a dull thud. 'Got a record we can try?'

Diana pulled out one of her boxed sets. He made a face. 'Let's have something a little lighter,' he said, selecting an old Beatles album.

Diana thought it sounded fine, but Oliver was apparently still not satisfied. He continued to fiddle with the back of the amplifier.

'Coffee's ready,' said Jenny, poking her head round the door.

'Not for me, thanks,' Oliver said. 'I've got to be getting back.'

'Already?' asked Diana.

''Fraid so,' he said. 'Did I tell you that something's come up? I can't make the weekend.'

'Oh, *Oliver*,' she scolded. 'I was looking forward to that.'

'So was I, darling. So was I. But duty calls. It'll all be over in less than a fortnight. Don't forget Venice. They won't be able to reach me there, and we'll have all the time in the world then.'

He kissed her, said goodbye to Jenny, and was gone.

Diana joined Jenny in the kitchen.

'I made myself some toast. Hope you don't mind.'

'Of course not.'

'Your boyfriend doesn't like me much, does he?'

'Don't say that,' said Diana. 'Of course he likes you. He's just a bit awkward with people he doesn't know.'

Jenny didn't look convinced, but she let the subject drop. 'Got any peanut butter and jelly?'

Diana shook her head. 'Just Marmite,' she said, setting the jar down on the table. Jenny unscrewed the cap and sniffed it suspiciously. Her gaze fell on Diana's hand. 'Say, where's that chunk of jewellery you had on yesterday? Did Oliver take it back already? *Jesus*. Diana, what did you do to *your hand*.'

Diana looked at her hand and sighed. She'd almost forgotten about the nightmare. But her aching knuckles reminded her. She told Jenny all about it.

'Jesus!' said Jenny. 'That must have been some dream.' She took a bite out of her toast. 'Real *Night of the Living Dead* stuff.'

'It was horrible, really scary,' said Diana. 'It didn't seem like a dream at all. And then when I thought I'd woken up, and he was *there* in my *bed* . . .'

'Yeeuuchhh!' said Jenny. 'Think of it. In bed with that slimeball. You must've been really freaked.'

'But the funny thing is,' Diana said, 'I still can't find my ring.'

'Well, you were wearing it yesterday, that's for sure. It must be here somewhere.'

'But where? I've looked all over the place.' Diana poured herself some more coffee. She had searched the flat, without success, while Oliver had been fixing the stereo.

'Maybe you sleepwalked,' Jenny said. 'Maybe you really did go down to the basement. You could have left the ring there.'

Diana looked doubtful. 'I couldn't have sleepwalked

through the door of the flat. And the door was definitely locked. Oliver had to use his keys to get in this morning. I don't think anyone could sleepwalk their way through a Yale and two mortices, could they?'

'Maybe you really did forget to lock the door after I'd gone,' Jenny suggested. 'That part of it might have been for real.'

Diana shook her head. 'No, I don't think so. I don't *do* that sort of thing; I'm too worried about burglars.'

'Well, you said we'd be going down into the basement anyway,' said Jenny, 'so howzabout checking it out? You never know, you might find your ring down there.'

'I hope so,' Diana said doubtfully. 'Oh God, what shall I do if we can't find it? Oliver will be furious.'

Jenny looked at her curiously. 'It's only a piece of jewellery,' she said. 'So what if it cost . . . what? A couple of hundred dollars?' She grinned.

Diana smiled back, a little uncomfortably. 'A bit more than that, actually.'

'Well, so what?' Jenny was adamant. 'If he loves you, he'll forgive you. He can always bump up the insurance claim.

Diana nodded, but she wasn't entirely convinced. Oliver wouldn't mind about the money, she was sure. It was just that . . . well, losing her engagement ring ten days before the wedding didn't seem like a terribly good omen.

She hunted around in one of the crates and drew out a torch. 'We might need this,' she said. 'It's dark down there.'

* * *

Diana almost lost her nerve when they got to the basement door. She clutched at Jenny's arm. 'I can't. What if the fat man's still down there? What if he really is dead?'

'Nah,' said Jenny. 'You're not dreaming now. At least,

I know *I'm* not. Come on. Trust me.' She opened the door.

Diana still hung back.

'Diana! Come *on*.'

'Yes,' said Diana, trying to convince herself. 'You're right. This is not a dream. This is real.'

'Of course it's real,' said Jenny. 'D'you think I'd stand for a supporting role in someone else's nightmare? Come on.'

She found the light switch, turned it on, and started down the steps. Diana touched the wall with her finger. It was cool, but dry. No hint of slime anywhere. Cautiously, she followed Jenny down.

The basement looked perfectly ordinary. It was nothing like the place in her dream. There were no passageways leading off, no bottomless pits, as far as she could see. It was just a room with pipes, a boiler and a load of old junk.

'What a blast,' said Jenny, delving into the nearest crate. 'It's like an antique shop down here. All this old stuff.'

'This is nothing like the place I dreamt about,' Diana said. 'This is just the normal basement.'

Jenny was digging like a terrier.

'Ring any bells?' Diana asked. She switched on the torch and started to comb the floor with the beam, hoping to catch sight of a telltale glitter.

'Not really,' Jenny said. 'Just a load of old picture frames. Shame there aren't any photos or anything. Hey, what's this?'

Diana looked up. 'Something you recognise?'

'Nah,' said Jenny. She brushed the dust from the cover of a large book, then flicked through some of the pages. 'But it sure is pretty. Looks like fairy-stories. Can we take it?'

'Of course,' Diana said. 'It doesn't belong to anyone

now.' The beam of her torch passed over the boiler, into the recess beyond, and over the tear-stained face of a little girl. She jumped in surprise. The torch dropped out of her hand and rolled across the floor.

'What's up?' asked Jenny.

'Nothing,' Diana said. She hadn't *really* seen it. She couldn't have done. She retrieved the torch and directed it back into the dark corner. Her mind was playing tricks again. Of course there was no little girl.

'I must be seeing things,' she said.

'What did you see?' asked Jenny. 'That photographer guy?'

'Yeah,' said a voice from behind her. 'Anybody seen my photographer lately?'

Jenny gave a shriek and threw herself towards Diana. Both girls stood cowering by the boiler, watching as a gaunt figure emerged from behind the up-ended pool table. It was the journalist, Paul Lawrence.

'You asshole!' Jenny exclaimed. 'You scared the shit out of me.'

Diana groaned as she saw who it was. Partly from annoyance, but partly from relief. He wasn't one of the walking dead, at least. He was all too real. 'What are *you* doing here?' she snapped.

'I'm looking for my lensman,' he said. 'I left him here last night. He hasn't been seen since.'

'Get out or we'll call the cops,' said Jenny.

'The *cops*? Go ahead, call them. But he's been here. I *know* he's been here.' He held out a roll of Kodak film. 'This belongs to him.'

'So what?' said Jenny.

'Yes,' said Diana. 'So what? Now get out of here!' She grabbed hold of Jenny's arm and pulled her towards the stairs. 'Go and get your stupid film developed!'

'I might just do that,' he said. He didn't seem as aggressive as yesterday. In fact, if Diana let herself think

76

about it, Paul Lawrence looked almost as anxious as she felt.

The girls reached the bottom of the steps, Jenny sprinted up two at a time.

'I haven't seen him,' said Diana. 'He hasn't been here.'

'Come *on*, Diana,' Jenny urged.

Diana climbed the steps. Paul Lawrence made no attempt to follow. He stood directly under the light, looking up at them. The low-watt bulb threw deep shadows across his face.

'You'd better get out of here, scumbag!' cried Jenny. She tugged impatiently at Diana's arm. 'Let's *go*, Di. We're getting out of here.'

Diana was in a daze. Jenny pushed her out into the hallway. 'And as for *you*,' she shouted back into the basement. 'If you're not out of here in one *minute*, you're going to be in *deep shit*, asshole!'

They went back into the flat. Diana stood and watched as Jenny shut the door and drew the bolt across. 'Keys,' she said. 'Where are the keys?' Diana produced them. Jenny double-locked the door.

'There. Now he can't get in, even if he tries.' She looked round. Diana had gone. Jenny found her sitting at the kitchen table, her head clutched in her hands.

'Hey, it's okay,' Jenny said. 'He's no problem. We'll just call the cops if he doesn't go away.'

'I'm not worried about *him*,' said Diana. 'It's the other one. Whatsisname. The photographer, Peck. Where *is* he?'

'Don't ask me,' said Jenny. 'He probably got bored and pissed off back to wherever he came from. Who cares?'

Diana took a deep breath. 'But don't you see? He's disappeared. I dreamt he fell into that pit, and now he's gone.'

'Hey,' said Jenny. 'We should be so lucky. Lard mountains like him don't vanish that easily. He's probably sitting in some sleazy burger bar, feeding his face with cholesterol.'

'I'm scared,' said Diana.

'Hey,' said Jenny, 'this dream business has really got you going, hasn't it?'

'It's not the only nightmare I've had recently,' Diana admitted. She told Jenny all she could remember of her recent dreams. Jenny nodded sympathetically.

'I guess you're going through a rough time,' she said at last. 'I have nightmares too, you know. Really freaky ones. Like I'm in this bar, and no one will serve me.'

'I've always had dreams,' said Diana. 'I dream a lot about a ruined city, but that's not a nightmare. It's like there's an estate agent showing me round, and I'm wondering whether to buy it or not. You know, this place is a mess, but with a bit of work . . . I'm thinking about whether I could live there, and whether or not Oliver will like it.'

Jenny laughed. 'You sound like a property developer!'

'And that's not all,' Diana said. Tentatively, afraid that Jenny would laugh again, she told her about the premonitions she had had as a child. Her grandfather falling down the steps of the wine cellar, and the more trivial occasions when she had dreamt precisely about what she was going to get for Christmas or birthdays.

'Mummy always thought I'd found her hiding places, because I always knew what the presents were going to be. She used to get cross, so after a while I learned to keep quiet about it.'

'Wow,' Jenny said. She was impressed. 'You don't dream like that any more?'

'No,' Diana said. 'I haven't had one of those for ages. The nearest I came to it was when I dreamt about a particular horse winning the Derby. I don't normally bet on things like that, but I persuaded Daddy to back it for me.'

'And?'

'It lost!' Diana said, a little ruefully. 'That was it, really. Whatever I'd had when I was little, I didn't have it any more.'

'Shame,' said Jenny. 'We could've had a ball at Caesar's Palace.'

Diana checked her watch. 'Would you like to stay for supper?'

'Sure. That'd be great.'

'It won't be much,' Diana said. 'The cooker's not working yet.'

'Doesn't matter,' said Jenny. 'We could call up for some pizzas or something.'

Diana shook her head. 'I don't think so. There aren't too many take-aways round here. But we can get some odds and ends from the shop down the road. And there's plenty of champagne in the fridge.'

'Yeah, neat,' said Jenny. 'Look, why don't you stay here. In case those guys are hanging around. I'll do the shopping. Just tell me how to get there. And how much it'll cost. I can't work out your English money.'

Diana made out a short list: bread, cheese and salami. 'And fruit, if they've got any.' She pressed a five pound note into Jenny's hand. 'That should be enough.'

Jenny saluted smartly. 'Yes, ma'am! Hoffman Door-to-Door Deliveries At Your Service!'

Diana let her out and locked the door behind her, slowly and deliberately, so that there would be no question in her mind that she had done it. She went back into the kitchen and noticed the book Jenny had brought up with her from the basement: *Favourite Fairy-Tales*. Intrigued, she sat down and turned to the contents page.

They might have been *somebody's* favourite fairy-tales, but they weren't hers. She'd never even heard of any of these. 'The Rose Garden', she read, 'The Lady on the Grey'; 'The Bird With the Crystal Plumage'. Not one of the titles was in the least bit familiar. She began to flick through the pages, pausing whenever she came to a picture. The illustrations were hand-tinted watercolours, exquisitely detailed, in the style of Arthur Rackham.

She stopped to examine one of the pictures more carefully. It showed a house in the middle of a forest glade, dwarfed by the dark trees around it. A wisp of smoke curled up from the chimney. A little girl stood on the front step, her arm raised to knock on the door. Diana looked closer. How odd. It looked like the little girl she'd thought she'd seen in the basement. Perhaps she'd looked at the book before, without really registering it. Perhaps the little girl's face had implanted itself in her subconscious.

Was it Little Red Riding Hood? Diana saw no sign of the wolf, and the little girl's cloak was not red but green. She was surrounded by rabbits and squirrels. Diana looked at the trees. Was she imagining things, or were there wild animals in there? There was a hint of movement, not actual movement, but movement suggested by the lines, and perhaps a suggestion of eyes peering out at the little girl. Oh-oh, she thought. Someone should let the little girl into the house. It wasn't safe for her to be wandering outside on her own.

She turned over a few pages. The next illustration was similar to the first, but here the house took up most of the page. The porch looked familiar; it looked a bit like the front of her own house.

The little girl now appeared to be tapping on a window. Diana could see something through the leaded panes, but the painting wasn't very clear at this point; there was only a blur of colour. But why was the little girl still outside the house? Whatever was lurking in the trees would be coming closer. She skimmed the page of type opposite, but the story seemed to bear no relation to the illustration. Diana leafed through the pages until she found the next picture.

This seemed to be a toyshop, or perhaps it was a nursery. There was a small window in the background. Diana could just about make out the face of the little girl, pressed up against the pane of glass, staring hungrily, like an orphan shut out in the cold while all the fun went on inside. Dolls, teddy bears, stuffed animals and wooden building blocks were crammed into the foreground. She looked more closely. That dolls' house wasn't a dolls' house after all, she realised. It was a face. If she looked *very* carefully, she could just about make out a figure lying amongst the toys. It was like the puzzles in the comic books she'd had as a child: spot the hidden man in the picture. The figure, she saw now, was grossly overweight, not realistic at all, and its head had been drawn at a very peculiar angle. But, if she squinted, she could just about make out the form of the dead photographer. There was blood coming out of his mouth. He leered at her, and winked.

Diana slammed the book shut. Her imagination was running riot again. She stared at the front cover for a full minute, then steeled herself to open it again. She flicked through nervously, then went through it again, turning the pages more slowly. But she still couldn't find the painting of the toys. All she could see were some boring pictures of a vast grey landscape. Losing patience, she closed the book firmly. It was all nonsense. She was overwrought.

She looked at her watch again. Jenny had only been gone for a few minutes, though it seemed like hours.

Diana decided to keep herself busy until Jenny's return. Sitting and brooding and imagining things wouldn't get her anywhere. She got to her feet . . .

And sat down again with a thump. She could have sworn that the floor had tilted, like the deck of a ship. She stared down at the vinyl tiles. Was it her imagination, or was the marbled pattern rippling like shallow waves on a beach? Impossible.

But the room *was* shaking. She turned round, alarmed. The cups were dancing on their hooks. Crockery chinked as it vibrated. Was it an earthquake? No, that was ridiculous. A tube train? No, the nearest station was a good fifteen minutes' walk away. The trains didn't pass through anywhere near here. She'd have felt them already if they did.

She braced herself against the back of the chair. The vibrations were getting stronger. A cup, half-filled with cold coffee, did a kamikaze leap off the table and shattered, sending brown liquid coursing across the floor. A china pig did a jig before throwing itself, lemming-like, from the shelf above the sink. Diana pulled herself to her feet and tottered towards the door, clinging to the edge of the table for support. It felt as though the whole room were on roller-skates.

There was a sound like a sheet being torn in half and a huge black crack snaked across the wall above her. Then there was a seething, whispering hiss. The crack bulged. Something was trying to climb through it. Diana saw the tips of fingers pushing their way through the disintegrating plaster. Long, dirty fingernails scraped at the wall.

She threw herself out of the kitchen and unlocked the door. She thought the vibrations might have stopped, but she was shaking so much she couldn't be sure. She ran through the hallway and out into the street. Jenny was rounding the corner with a carrier bag. She looked on amazed as Diana lurched towards her, shouting and waving her arms like a mad person.

'Hey! What happened? You look like you saw a ghost.'

'The flat . . .' panted Diana. 'I don't know. It was shaking. It started to crack up.'

She looked around her suspiciously. There was no sign that anything unusual had happened out here. No cracks in the pavement. No wrecked cars. Not even any toppled trees.

'Sounds like an earth tremor,' said Jenny. 'I didn't feel anything, but then you don't feel it so much when you're out walking.'

'We don't get earthquakes in London,' Diana protested. 'It's not like California.'

Jenny shrugged. 'Whatever it was, it's over now.'

She led Diana back into the flat. Everything seemed normal. Diana was beginning to think her imagination had gone into overdrive again. She was almost relieved when they found the kitchen in a shambles. Cutlery and smashed plates littered the floor.

'Will you look at this,' Jenny said, awestruck. She was examining the crack in the wall. 'You *did* have an earthquake in here. Maybe you're giving the house nightmares now.'

'There was something trying to get through,' Diana said. 'I know it sounds silly,' she added lamely. It did sound silly; the crack was too narrow for fingers. She sighed. 'I'd just got the kitchen straightened out, as well.'

'I'll give you a hand tidying up,' said Jenny, picking a large piece of china off the floor. 'You don't suppose the house is on a faultline, do you?'

'Subsidence? That's all we need. Damn those surveyors.'

'You look whacked,' said Jenny. 'You need a drink. Better crack open one of those big green bottles you keep in the fridge.' She began to unload the contents of her carrier bag onto the table. 'Look what I've got you,' she said.

Diana looked, and made a face. Jenny was holding up a cheap glass ashtray. 'I don't care if this *is* a No Smoking Zone,' she said. 'I need a cigarette as well as a drink.'

*   *   *

'Listen to this,' said Jenny. 'It says that the crack is a sexual symbol.'

She was thumbing through the dictionary of dreams. Diana had bought it the day before. She'd looked at it for a few minutes, then thrown it down in annoyance. It was trivial and silly: no use to her at all. But Jenny was obviously amused by it.

Diana giggled. 'According to that book, *everything* is a sexual symbol.'

Jenny flicked through some more of the pages. 'You're right,' she said. 'Wedding rings: they're sexual too.'

'I didn't dream about a *wedding* ring,' said Diana. ' I dreamt about my *engagement* ring.'

'Yeah, yeah, yeah. Same thing, I guess,' said Jenny. She took the champagne bottle and turned it upside-down over her glass. A few drops fell out. 'I don't suppose you've got any more of this stuff?'

''Course,' said Diana. 'Hang on a minute.' She disappeared into the kitchen to replenish supplies.

Jenny pointed the remote control at the television to turn the sound up. A pompous-looking man was speaking: '. . . has resulted in nothing more than a monopoly, offering a shamefully substandard service at prices that are no longer competitive . . .'

'Hear, hear,' said a woman with spectacles, nodding sagely, 'What's the point in co-opting all this talent when the structure of the company is in such disarray? This is going to blow up in our faces. We should have waited.'

There was a little girl sitting next to the woman. Now her childish voice piped up. 'It's all right for *you*,' she whined. 'Some of us are stuck in a format completely alien to our natural proclivities. Get it over with as quickly as we can. That's what I say.'

'Precisely,' said another man, mopping his fat face with a handkerchief as he talked. 'Angela's right. Get this business out of the way, and then, when we go public, we'll have all the more leverage . . .'

Jenny turned the sound down again. 'Jeez,' she said as Diana came back into the room with another bottle. 'English TV has to be the most boring thing on earth.'

'What's that?' Diana asked, sitting down again.

'Nothing,' said Jenny, turning back to the book. 'This is crap. It says here that dreaming about werewolves means you're frightened of men. I've had loads of dreams about werewolves, and *I'm* not frightened of men.'

'What does it say about maggots?' Diana asked, shuddering at the memory.

Jenny looked it up. 'Sex, all sex,' she said. 'Let's face it, Diana. You're sex mad.'

'No, I'm not,' said Diana.

'Come on, Di. The shy, English rose type? You're just a seething mass of sensuality under that cool blonde exterior. I'll bet you turn into a superslut once you're in bed. Hey, you're blushing! Hey, that's real cute!'

'No, it's not,' said Diana, trying to hide her face with her hair. 'And I'm not. I mean, I don't. I haven't.'

'You haven't what? Done it, you mean? Come off it, Diana. You can't be serious.'

'Well why not? What's wrong with that?' Diana became defensive. She was used to fading quietly into the background whenever her friends talked about their sexual experiences, when they started to giggle and swap stories about getting tipsy and ending up in bed.

'Nothing wrong with it,' said Jenny. 'I just . . . I cannot believe that you're . . . how old are you? Have you ever kissed a guy?'

'Of course I have,' Diana retorted. She had kissed Oliver, many times. And before that, there had been a man, much older than herself, at a party. She had never known his name. And then there had been that awful stablehand. But he didn't count . . .

'But you've never . . . been to bed . . . done *it* . . .?' Jenny's voice petered out in wonderment.

'So?' Diana stuck her chin out defiantly.

Jenny gave out a long, low whistle. 'No kidding. Don't get me wrong, I think it's great. And pretty smart, too. Especially with AIDS and everything. But no wonder you're having these dreams. Marriage is a real big deal for you, then. If you've never had sex before, I mean.'

There was an embarrassed silence. Jenny was relieved when Diana burst out laughing. 'So that's what it's all about!' said Diana. 'Sexual anxiety! That's why I'm having nightmares!'

'Maybe,' Jenny said. She lit another cigarette.

Diana wrinkled her nose, but said nothing. She would have to open all the windows in the morning to get the smell of the smoke out of the room. She made up her mind to have a word with Jenny about it. But not yet. Not now. She didn't want to spoil the evening.

'I never thought of myself as a neurotic spinster,' she said at last.

'You're not neurotic,' said Jenny. 'You're just a normal person leading an abnormal life. I mean, your lifestyle isn't exactly typical, you know.'

'Lifestyle?' said Diana, puzzled. 'What lifestyle?'

'Lifestyles of the Rich and Famous,' said Jenny. 'You're a celebrity. Well, almost. Your pop's rolling in it, and you get pestered by reporters. That's pretty wacko for starters. Hold it, let's see what the book says about photographers. Cameras are phallic symbols, that's for sure.'

'Give me that!' said Diana, laughing, as she made a grab for the paperback. Jenny rolled onto her back, holding the book out of Diana's reach. 'No, I don't think you should be allowed to read this. It's *lewd*. Hey, check out the TV.'

Diana looked at the screen. It was a couple of comedians. One was fat and the other thin. They reminded her of . . .

'No, it's not them,' she said. 'It only looks like them.'

'They stink,' Jenny said. 'I saw them on TV the other night. Come to think of it, they *do* look a bit like . . .' She turned up the sound on the television.

'And you know what?' the fat man was saying. 'I've still got the engagement ring!' There was a roar of laughter from the studio audience.

'Noooh!' explained the thin man. 'Really?'

Diana snatched the remote control and switched the set off. She sat staring at the blank screen, suddenly plunged into depression.

'Shall I put the radio on?' Jenny asked.

Diana shook her head. She studied her hands nervously. 'Look, I don't suppose you could stay the night, could you?' she asked at last. 'It's getting late, and you shouldn't really be travelling on the tube at this hour.'

'Sure,' said Jenny. Travelling on the night train didn't worry her at all, but she could see that Diana wanted her to stay. 'I don't mind hanging around. You look as though you could do with company.'

'I really don't want to go to sleep tonight,' Diana said. 'I really don't think I could take another of those awful dreams.'

'No problem,' said Jenny. 'We'll make an all-nighter out of it. A slumber-free slumber party, with lots of strong black coffee.' She scrambled to her feet and headed for the kitchen. 'I'll go put the water on.'

'Don't forget we've got a bottle of pop to finish off,' Diana called after her.

'Right,' Jenny yelled back. 'Hey, I forgot all about *this*.' She came back into the lounge with the book of fairy-tales.

'I was looking at that earlier,' Diana said. 'It's a very peculiar book.'

'*I'll* say,' said Jenny, looking through it. 'No pictures. I could have sworn it had pictures before.'

87

'But it *did* have pictures,' said Diana. 'I know it did.' She looked at the book over Jenny's shoulder. Page after page consisted of nothing but print.

*　　*　　*

Jenny opened her eyes. She was curled up on the floor. There was a bitter taste in her mouth. She sat up, trying to work out where she was.

Then it all came back to her. The coffee hadn't done the trick. She had crashed out, after all. Too much champagne. She took a look around. The lounge looked as if a bomb had hit it. The floor was covered with bottles, breadcrumbs, cheese crusts and salami rind. The ashtray was overflowing with cigarette ends. Books and records were scattered all over the place.

She saw a hideous china doll grinning at her from one of the shelves. Half of its face was missing. It looked ancient. Probably some sort of antique, Jenny thought. Funny she hadn't noticed it before.

Diana was nowhere to be seen.

Jenny picked up the jug and knocked back a mouthful of coffee. It was cold. It tasted disgusting. Slowly, feeling a major-league headache revving up in her cranium, she got to her feet. 'Diana?'

She checked the rest of the flat. Diana wasn't in the bedroom. Nor was she in the kitchen. Jenny felt uneasy. Maybe Diana was sleepwalking again. She gulped down a glass of water at the sink, then headed back towards the lounge. Diana couldn't have simply disappeared. She had to be *somewhere*.

As Jenny emerged from the kitchen, she noticed that the front door had been left ajar. She frowned. Had Diana gone out? What was she thinking of, leaving the door open like that? Especially with those reporter guys still hanging around.

88

'Diana?' Jenny peered into the hallway. It was dark, and the shadows were empty. Neither Diana nor anyone else was there.

There was a noise. It came from somewhere beneath her feet. It sounded like a scraping, like something being dragged across the floor of the basement. Maybe Diana was down there. Jenny locked up and thrust the keys deep into the pocket of her jeans.

'Diana? You down there?' she said, not daring to raise her voice too much. It *had* to be Diana, she thought. There was no one else in the house. Diana had said so.

She went along the hallway. The door to the basement was open. She felt for the light switch. It wasn't where she remembered it. It wasn't anywhere to be found.

'Diana!' she called, louder this time. There was another noise from below. This one sounded like a door slamming. Jenny couldn't remember seeing any doors down in the basement, but then she hadn't had a chance to look around it properly.

She made up her mind. She went down.

And descended into another world. The basement wasn't like she remembered it at all. But neither was it the cavern that Diana had described from her dream.

She was standing at one end of a corridor lined with doors. The whole place looked like it needed decorating. The carpet beneath her feet was threadbare and dirty. The wallpaper was peeling. The paint on the doors was brown and cracked. Somewhere, a clock was ticking.

There was a small printed sign on the nearest door. It said, simply: 'Pursuit'. Jenny tried the doorknob. For some reason, she was relieved that it wouldn't turn. She moved cautiously along the corridor, trying the doors as she went. None of them would open, though she thought she could hear voices murmuring behind one or two.

The feeling of unease grew. Something was wrong here. Something was very wrong. She made herself try one more doorknob before turning to go back. She retraced her steps, but the corridor seemed to have no beginning and no end. There were no steps leading up to and out of the basement. There were no steps at all.

Where the hell am I? she thought.

Going down into the basement had been a *bad* idea. She knew that now. She should have realised it earlier. She had seen enough horror movies to know that characters should *never* go down into the basement on their own. Especially in places like this. Especially at night.

It was no use remembering that now. Now she was stuck in this awful corridor. Maybe this was someone's apartment. Maybe she had found her way next door by mistake, taken the wrong stairs or something. Technically, she supposed, that would mean she was trespassing. She didn't fancy being caught by whoever lived here. But, on the other hand, at least if they found her they'd be able to show her the way out.

A door slammed behind her. There was a pattering of footsteps. Jenny whirled round. A small figure in a white dress was running away from her down the corridor. It looked like a little girl.

'Hey!' said Jenny. 'Wait!'

The little girl seemed not to hear. She disappeared through one of the doors, leaving it open. Jenny sprinted after her.

When she reached the door, she stopped and stared. The room hardly looked lived in. Everything was covered with a thick layer of dust. Huge white shapes loomed up out of the gloom. Jenny saw that the shapes were furniture, covered with sheets. There was a bow window on the far wall, but, beyond it, only darkness.

The little girl was sitting in front of an enormous dressing table. She had very pretty hair. It was pale yellow, and it hung down her back in waves.

The mirror was covered with brown patches where the

silvering had worn away, but Jenny could just about see the little girl's face.

She'd seen that face before. She couldn't remember where, but she knew she'd seen it.

The little girl was playing with an old china doll. Its face was cracked. It was dressed in a tattered yellow frock. Jenny thought she recognised the doll, too. It was the ugliest doll she had ever seen.

'Little girl!' she called softly, not wanting to frighten the child. 'Hey, little girl!'

The child gave no sign of having heard her. She continued to play with the doll, smoothing its shock of hair and straightening its frock, talking to it in a gentle voice. 'Sleep now,' she said, closing its eyes with her fingers. 'Go to sleep now, baby. Mummy'll wake you up in the morning.'

There was a small casket open on the dressing table. As Jenny watched, the little girl pulled out a long necklace of pearls and coiled them lovingly around the doll's neck. Then she pulled the necklace very tight. The doll's neck snapped sideways.

Jenny was on the point of stepping into the room when she sensed someone behind her. She turned. Along the corridor, a long way down the corridor, she could see the figure of a man. At first, he didn't seem to be moving, but then she realised it was a trick of the perspective. He was moving towards her. He was moving quite fast. Running.

Jenny gasped. She didn't know who the man was, but she didn't like him. She was scared of the man. She didn't want him to see her. She tried to move, but her limbs refused to obey the commands from her brain. She was frozen to the spot.

And the man was almost upon her. Jenny frantically sifted through the excuses in her head. She would say that she'd heard a sound, come down into the basement to investigate, got lost. No, she'd say she was looking for Diana. Or she could say that . . .

Someone had given her permission?

And then it was too late for excuses, because the man was almost on top of her. Here he was. She caught a glimpse of eyes behind a pair of wide-rimmed spectacles, thick-lensed like the bottom of Coca-Cola bottles. His eyes were very pale, and staring, and the distortion made them look quite mad.

'I . . .' Jenny stuttered, but the man gave her no time. He ran straight through her, and hurtled into the room.

Jenny reeled against the door jamb, feeling dizzy. He hadn't even noticed her. It was as though she wasn't even there.

The man towered to a halt over the little girl. She shrank from him in fear.

'Don't you smile at me!' he shouted. His voice was very loud, and booming. It went through Jenny like a rumble of thunder.

The little girl wasn't smiling. Not at all. She looked terrified. 'It wasn't me!' she shouted. 'It was Angela!'

'And don't give me any more of that Angela nonsense!' boomed the man. 'You think you can get away with it! Well, you can't! You're coming with me!'

The little girl shouted back, her voice thin and piping: 'No!' She dropped the doll and backed away from him. 'I won't!'

The man lowered his voice. 'Oh yes you *will*, young miss. And no messing around. You're to come with me this instant!' He raised his arm. Jenny saw with horror that he was going to strike the little girl.

'Leave her alone!' she yelled. But neither of them seemed to hear her.

His hand came down, but the little girl dodged sideways and he missed. She twisted, then dropped to her knees and dived beneath one of the dustsheets.

The man stood for a moment, thinking. Then he stooped. He lifted the corner of the nearest dustsheet and peered underneath. Jenny could hear a scrabbling sound as the little girl scurried further away from him.

'Come out,' he wheedled, in the sort of voice that adults used when they joined in children's games. 'Come out, wherever you are!'

'No!' said a muffled voice. 'I won't!'

Jenny was furious with him. He had no right to scare the kid like that. She stepped forward and whisked the dustsheet out of the man's hand.

He looked round, surprised. But still he gave no sign of having seen her. Jenny felt as if she were invisible.

The man dropped to his knees and squinted along the ground. His face erupted into a broad smile, but the smile looked forced, strained. He didn't look at all happy.

'Come to daddy,' he said. 'Daddy's got a nice surprise for you.'

No, Jenny. *Don't* come to daddy. She looked around desperately. There had to be *some* way she could disrupt this horrible little charade.

Her eye fell on the doll. She poked at it with her finger; it felt solid enough beneath her touch. She picked it up and yanked at the necklace coiled round its neck, trying to loosen it. The string broke and the pearls scattered, rolling all over the floor.

The man whirled round at the noise. There was puzzlement on his face, then a slow dawning of understanding. He could see her now, Jenny realised. Oh Jesus. He could see her now. She wished he couldn't.

He seemed to have forgotten all about the little girl. He was looking at Jenny now, advancing towards her with his arms outstretched.

'Come to daddy,' he said.

'You've got to be kidding,' said Jenny. She did exactly as the little girl had done. She dodged away from him bruising her hip on the corner of a covered table. She barely noticed the pain. She dropped to the floor on her hands and knees.

There were too many table-legs in the way. She scrabbled in the dust. A hand shot out and grabbed at her ankle. She rolled sideways under one of the dustsheets. She lay there, panting, keeping an eye on the paint-spattered sandals that were coming across the floor towards her.

'Come out, you little shit!' the man shouted. 'Come *out*!'

He was losing his cool. Jenny tried desperately to hang onto hers. She wormed on her stomach until her progress was barred by what looked like the base of an old wardrobe. Everything looked different from down here. It was a little girl's eye-view. She twisted her head, trying to spot the little girl, but the little girl was nowhere to be seen. Jenny felt glad for her. She, at least, had managed to get away.

There was the scraping noise of furniture being dragged across the floor. Then a slow tread. Coming nearer. Jenny tried not to breathe. The sheet nearest to her twitched. The man was bending down. She could see a bulky shape outlined against the cloth.

Jenny was terrified. *Diana*, she thought. *Where are you, Diana? Help me.*

'You've been a very . . . bad . . . girl . . .'

She clutched at the dustsheet. It was lifted out of her grasp. She *had* been a bad girl. And now he was going to punish her.

'A *very* bad girl.' She smelled something which reminded her, fleetingly, of Chinatown. Then she forced herself to look up at the face.

It wasn't the man in glasses at all. It was the photographer. It was Peck.

He looked dreadful. His skin was puffy, tinged with purple. There was dried brown stuff smeared around his mouth, and he seemed to be having a great deal of trouble keeping his tongue under control. It was lolling out, wetting his chin with saliva. Worst of all, he was smiling, or trying to. It was difficult to smile when half his mouth had been eaten away.

'No *way*,' said Jenny. 'This can't be for real.' She tried to back away on her hands and knees. The wardrobe stopped her.

A pudgy hand was groping in her direction. Jenny squirmed as it plucked at her sleeve.

This couldn't be happening. This had to be a nightmare. She screwed her eyes shut.

All sounds faded. This was a bad dream. She would wake up in Diana's flat. Diana would be there. Everything would be back to normal.

Time passed. Civilisations rose from the land and crumbled back into dust. Jenny's eyes flickered open.

Peck's face filled her vision like a misshapen gourd. 'Peek-a-boo!' he chuckled, licking what remained of his discoloured lips with the swollen tongue.

Then he fastened his hands around her neck and began to squeeze.

Jenny felt herself going under. Black shapes flashed before her eyes. There was a roaring in her ears. Her lungs felt as though they were about to explode.

This was all wrong, she thought. Dreams didn't *hurt* like this.

She remembered her self-defence classes. She poked at his eyes with her fingers. She felt something pop, like an overripe grape, but his grip on her tightened. Her hand clawed at his face. The flesh felt like soft dough, wet and slippery. Her fingers fastened on something: an ear. She wrenched at it. It came off in her hand.

'Yeeeuuchhh!' the fat man squealed, clutching at the side of his head as he fell away from her. 'Jesus Christ! Fucking American tart!'

Jenny rolled clear of the dustsheets. For a moment she

stared, aghast, at what was in her hand. Then she flung it to the floor in revulsion.

Peck was still clutching at his head. Red jelly was oozing from between his fingers. Greyish-green matter was trickling from his ruined eye.

Jenny didn't wait any longer. She launched herself at the door, banging it shut behind her.

The corridor was completely dark, but she took it full tilt, not daring to pause for breath. There was something mushy underfoot. She slid sideways, but managed to stay on her feet.

Behind her, there was the crash of furniture being overturned. And the skittering noise of claws sliding off polished wood. Peck started to yodel. It sounded like a hunting call.

She found herself at the bottom of some steps. There were footsteps somewhere behind her in the dark. And a hoarse wheezing. The smell she had smelt earlier was stronger now. It hit her in waves.

She stumbled upwards and found her way blocked by a door.

Let this be a way out, she prayed. Please let this be a way out. Her hands found a doorknob. She turned it, and found herself in the hallway. She dug into her pocket for Diana's keys. But which one fitted which lock? It wasn't the first, nor the second . . .

Peck burst through the basement door as the third key slid into the lock and turned. She pulled the door open, darted through and slammed it shut behind her. She reached for the bolts and drew them across. Something crashed against the other side of the door. It bowed under the impact. She heard a small but ominous sound of splintering wood.

She backed into the lounge, watching wide-eyed as the door bulged beneath another blow.

There was a noise from the sofa behind her. She turned.

Diana's eyes were closed. She was curled up in a knot, her hands bunched tightly into fists. She was hitting out at something which Jenny couldn't see.

'Wake up!' Jenny yelled, leaping across the room. There was another crash at the door. Diana's whole body jolted as though she had had an electric shock.

'Diana!' Jenny shouted. 'Wake up!' She seized Diana's shoulder and shook her roughly. 'Wake up! For God's sake! *Wake up!*'

Diana's eyes snapped open. Her mouth opened too, but no sound came out of it. She clutched wildly at Jenny.

The pounding on the front door ceased. There was the faint sound of howling, fading into the distance. It might have been the wind.

'Jenny, I . . .' Diana was gasping for air. 'It was Peck. He . . . he was trying to break the door down . . . He was trying to get *in*.'

'I know,' said Jenny. 'I was *there*. He was after *me*.'

'You were . . .' Diana was still fighting her way out of the nightmare. She sat up suddenly. 'I was dreaming about you. There was a little girl, and . . .'

'I know,' Jenny repeated. 'I know. It's not possible, but I was there. You were dreaming about *me*. I was *in* your dream. It was *happening*.'

Diana stared at her. 'Then . . . you . . .'

'Yes,' said Jenny. 'I saw him. Peck was after *me*.' She touched her throat. It was still sore. 'He almost *got* me.'

Diana leaned forward. 'My God,' she breathed. 'There are bruises all over your neck.'

They looked at each other in silence. Diana brought her hand up and looked at the scraped skin on her knuckles.

'If I hadn't woken you up . . .' Jenny said slowly. 'If he had gotten into the apartment, what would have happened? What would have happened to *me*?'

They thought about it.

FRIDAY

'Hmmm,' said Deborah. 'Interesting.' She drummed her fingers on the table, looking down at the notes she'd been taking.

Diana almost lost patience with her. 'It may be interesting to you, but it's life or death to us.'

'Cool it, Di,' Jenny said, patting her on the arm. Deborah's trained eye lit automatically on this brief moment of body contact and filed it away as something to be considered at a later date. The girls had obviously achieved an instant rapport, but it didn't seem logical. Their backgrounds, behaviour, appearance and speech patterns were about as different as you could possibly get. Deborah had known Diana for three years now. Jenny didn't seem her type at all.

Perhaps, she thought, they were alter-egos, two different sides of the same personality. After all, they seemed to be sharing some sort of psychic experience. Alter-egos, yes. Deborah was pleased with this concept and listened with a new attentiveness. And, for the umpteenth time, she silently cursed the men who had cut off her research grant.

'There must be some sort of scientific explanation,' ventured Diana.

'I agree,' said Deborah. 'But even scientists, these days, are having to acknowledge that there are areas of experience that cannot be easily incorporated into what they know of the material world. Astral projection, for example, or ESP . . .'

Now it was Jenny's turn to get rattled. 'Hold it a minute, doc. All this astral stuff is bullshit. We weren't on drugs, we were totally straight. Okay, so we'd got a couple of pints of champagne in us. But we were both standing up, coherent.'

'I'm sure you were,' said Deborah. 'I didn't mean to belittle what must have been a genuinely frightening experience for the both of you.'

'And how do you explain Jenny's neck? And my hand?' asked Diana.

'I have one or two theories about that,' Deborah said. 'I don't really want to go into them now. We should stick to one thing at a time.'

'Yeah,' Jenny muttered under her breath. 'She probably thinks I tried to throttle myself.' Diana kicked her under the table. Deborah was only trying to help, after all. And, well, their story *did* seem a little farfetched.

'It seems to me,' Deborah said slowly, 'that each of you has found in the other a sort of *soulmate*, if you like. An amalgam of all those elements in which your respective characters and lives are lacking. I don't mean, of course, that you're lacking as *people*, just that none of us can be all things at once. Somehow, you've managed to link up, like two halves of a molecule, and the synthesis has resulted in something foreign to your everyday experience. Your perceptions have been turned inside-out.'

'Mmm,' said Diana.

'Yeah,' said Jenny. Neither of them liked to admit they didn't have the first clue as to what Deborah was going on about. *Psychospeak*, Jenny termed it. Diana still had the uneasy feeling that Deborah was viewing her as a case history instead of a person, perhaps as fascinating material for a ground-breaking thesis on dream therapy as treatment for mental disorder.

Deborah studied their expressions. 'I can see I'm not helping very much,' she admitted.

'Don't say that,' said Diana. 'You're the only person we can talk to.'

'Hmmm,' said Deborah. 'That in itself is indicative of something, I suppose. Do you not think that Oliver would be willing to listen? All this is so obviously a symptom of your anxieties about the wedding. Talking to him might get it off your chest.'

'I've already talked to him,' said Diana. 'About the nightmares, I mean.'

'And?'

'And he told me not to worry,' Diana said.

'So she's all uptight about getting hitched,' said Jenny. 'So where does that leave me?'

'To tell you the truth, Jenny, I don't really know,' said Deborah. 'Except that perhaps it's got something to do with the fact that you've lived in the house before. Subliminal memories can produce incredibly strong impressions on the psyche. All your nerve-endings are out there, waving, ready to pick up the slightest signal from Diana's subconscious. And we already know,' here she smiled at Diana, 'that her subconscious shows signs of exceptional development. All those dreams as a child.'

'The little girl in the dream last night,' Jenny said. 'I thought I knew her. I think I saw her on television. And the doll was the same as the one in Diana's apartment.'

'There you are,' said Deborah triumphantly. 'You've both of you been incorporating everyday impressions into these dreams of yours.'

She stood up. 'I've really got to get moving, I'm afraid. They're bringing in a kid who's disembowelled his pet hamster. Pretty nasty case.'

She picked up her notepad. 'I'm sorry I can't be more helpful. This is basically something that you'll have to see through on your own, you know. It's a case of confronting your own fears, dredging up memories that perhaps you'd rather not think about. All I can offer is objective advice.'

'Which is . . .?' asked Jenny. Privately, she found Deborah no help at all, but she could sense that Diana was feeling better, even though her face was smudged with fatigue.

'Get hold of a camera,' said Deborah. 'Keep it with you at all times. Go down into the basement. Photograph whatever you see. Either you'll end up with visual proof that there's nothing to be afraid of, that bricks and mortar are solid things that can't possibly change their shape. Or . . .'

Her voice trailed off.

Or what? Jenny wanted to say.

'Just do it,' Deborah said.

* * *

'You'd better take it,' said Diana. 'I'm no good with technical things.'

Jenny prised the camera out of its polystyrene wrapping. The accompanying manual was written in Japanese, Arabic, Spanish, French and German. She eventually found half a page of English and a series of diagrams, top-heavy with arrows and bad graphics. It looked like a war zone. Jenny scanned it for a minute, then gave up and threw it across the room.

'Seems simple enough,' she said, examining the camera. 'You just stick the batteries in *here*, put *that* in *there*. And press *here*.'

The flash went off in Diana's face. She squealed and tried to cuff Jenny around the ear. 'You're getting as bad as the fat man,' she said. 'Flashing in my face all the time.'

Jenny doubled up with laughter, but the thought of the

photographer seemed to sober Diana up. Jenny saw her mouth sagging, and waved the developing print at her as a distraction. 'Let's see how photogenic you are.'

'Oh, I'm *very* photogenic,' Diana said. 'I come from a long line of people who were always having their photographs taken.'

'And before that they were having their portraits painted by Leonardo da Vinci,' Jenny added.

'That's right,' Diana grinned. 'We're all terrific poseurs in our family. We're in all the best magazines, you know.'

'I had my picture in a paper once,' Jenny said. 'I was in the front row at a Jon Bon Jovi gig.'

'A *what?*' asked Diana. Jenny measured the culture gap and saw that it was probably too wide to bridge at this particular point. 'Oh, nothing important,' she said. 'You could only make out part of my forehead anyway.'

'Well, you're no David Bailey,' said Diana, eyeing the image that was gradually emerging from the print. Her mouth was open, her eyeballs were red and the outlines of her face were fuzzy.

'You should've bought a better camera then,' Jenny said. 'Instead of this cheap plastic job.' She took the print and looked at it. 'Oh, I don't know. I think it's kinda artistic, don't you?'

'So!' Diana said, drawing a deep breath. 'What shall we do now? Do we go down into the basement, or what?'

'I guess so,' said Jenny. 'D'you really think anything'll happen? I mean, neither of us is asleep. As far as I can make out.'

'It's now or never,' said Diana. She picked up the torch and switched it on.

'Yeah. Let's do it.'

They did it. They went down. The basement was waiting for them. It was back to its normal self. Whatever tricks it might have had up its sleeve, it wasn't showing them.

'It's funny,' Diana said. 'I hate basements. It reminds me of when my grandfather . . . you know . . . But I seem to be spending an awful lot of time in this one.' She reached the bottom of the steps and struck out into the farmost shadowy reaches.

'Face your fears,' said Jenny. 'That's what your buddy Deborah said, wasn't it? Confront your nightmares in the flesh.'

'I'd rather not, if you don't mind,' Diana said. 'Especially if they're all like Peck.'

'Well, everything looks normal now,' said Jenny.

'No secret passageways,' said Diana. 'No bottomless pit.'

Both of them heard the noise at the same time.

They exchanged glances. It was the faint but unmistakable sound of a child sobbing.

'Yep, I hear it,' Jenny said in reply to Diana's unspoken question. 'What do we do now? We can't photograph a noise.'

'Where's it coming from?'

'Over there,' said Jenny, pointing. 'No, over *there*. No . . .'

It was all around them. It seemed to be coming from the very walls of the basement.

Then, a small voice: 'Help me.' The sobbing faded into silence.

'Shit,' said Jenny. 'This is too weird.'

'It was probably just a neighbour's kid,' Diana suggested. 'The acoustics can sometimes be peculiar in these old places.'

Jenny just looked at her. She didn't bother to say anything. Neither of them believed Diana's explanation for one minute.

'What'll we do?'

'Follow the noise to its source,' Diana said, sounding braver than she felt.

'But it was coming from the walls . . .'

'Then we examine the walls,' Diana said, lighting their way with the torch. Jenny followed, camera held at the ready.

'Sure, let's examine the walls,' she repeated. 'If we can find them . . .'

They couldn't be sure of exactly when it had happened. There was no sudden movement. There was just a minor shift of perspective at the corner of their vision, a change that took place in the blinking of an eye. The basement had expanded.

Now there was a wide, brick-lined passageway which stretched as far as they could see, disappearing into distant shadow.

Diana looked back. She wasn't sure, but she thought she could just about make out the basement steps. They were a long, long way away. Even as she looked, they seemed to shimmer and dissolve.

'Looks like our line of retreat has been cut off,' said Jenny. She'd been following Diana's gaze. 'We've got to see this thing through, remember?'

Diana nodded. 'The power of positive thinking,' she muttered. 'Take a picture, Jenny. Let's see if it photographs.'

Jenny obediently pressed the shutter. The flash dazzled them for an instant, illuminating the cavernous space before they were plunged back into gloom.

'So what's next?' asked Diana.

'Well, let's not hang around waiting for the next party piece,' said Jenny. 'Let's *go*.' She pointed down the tunnel.

They linked arms and advanced.

The passageway twisted and turned until they'd lost all sense of direction. Pipes and clumps of cable ran along the ceiling, occasionally disappearing into holes crusted with orange mould, or reappearing to run on again.

Noises came and went as they walked. Sometimes they

heard small scrabbling sounds, like tiny claws scratching against sheet metal. But they never saw any rats, something for which both girls were profoundly grateful. Sometimes they would hear the low rumble of distant machinery. Once, Diana could have sworn, she caught the murmur of a large crowd, and a voice, loud and clear above the rest, saying: 'Now you've received your diplomas and you know what's expected of you. I want you to go out there, girls and boys, and knock them dead. Give them *hell*.'

'Did you hear that?' she asked Jenny.

'What? You mean the growling?'

Diana shook her head. 'Forget it,' she said.

This was the place she had dreamt about, but it was somehow different from her nightmare. It had changed. Or perhaps *she* had changed. The basement was a witches' kitchen, she decided. A dream factory. A place where weird nightmares were cooked up, ready to be foisted on some impressionable sleeper.

But did it really exist, or was she dreaming it?

'Pinch me,' she said to Jenny. 'Tell me I'm awake.'

'You're awake,' said Jenny. 'I wish you weren't.'

Diana decided she had imagined the sound of the crowd. But she wasn't imagining the music that was drifting down the corridor towards them. Jenny gripped Diana's arm tightly. She could hear it too.

It was the tinkling of a distant piano.

The passage sloped upwards, then turned a sharp corner. There was a dead end up ahead: a wall of solid-looking brick. There was a door embedded in the wall, looking as though it didn't really belong there. It was slightly ajar. Light spilled out through the crack. The piano music was coming from somewhere inside.

'Have we been here before?' asked Jenny. 'I know that door from somewhere.'

'Me too,' Diana said. Then she recognised it.

'It's the door to my flat,' she said.

'No!' said Jenny.

'Yes,' said Diana. 'It *is*. But it's different.'

'What's it doing down here?'

'Damned if I know,' said Diana. She went up to the door and pushed it open. Not knowing quite what to expect, she went inside.

'Do not pass go,' muttered Jenny. 'Do not collect two hundred dollars.' She followed Diana in.

Diana turned left, to where her bedroom should have been. But her bedroom wasn't there. She found herself in the lounge.

'I don't believe it,' she said.

'You've got to be kidding,' said Jenny.

They were in Diana's flat all right. The lounge was an almost perfect replica. Almost, but not quite. Whoever had tried to copy it had got something wrong.

Diana's first thought was: 'But it's so *tidy*.'

Jenny went into the kitchen. 'There's no crack in the wall,' she called. 'And no broken plates.' She came back into the lounge. 'This is weird. What's wrong here? There's something wrong.'

'It's back-to-front,' Diana said. 'Like *Through the Looking-Glass*.' She picked up a magazine. It was a copy of *NEEUQ & SREPRAH*.

'Not *this* looking-glass,' said Jenny. She walked over to the mantelpiece where the radio perched, still giving out the piano music they had heard in the passageway. The frame on the wall indicated where the mirror should have been, but instead of their reflections there was a dense black nothingness.

'I can't see my reflection,' whispered Jenny. 'Maybe we're vampires.'

'No,' said Diana. 'There's no reflection of *anything*.'

It was true. The mirror was a black hole. No reflected image, no glass. Nothing. It looked capable of swallowing them up. Not just them, but the whole room.

Diana stretched out a hand and touched the blackness. Her fingertips disappeared into it. She jerked her arm back in alarm.

'It's freezing cold,' she said, blowing on her fingers to warm them up.

'I don't like this,' Jenny said. 'Where are we? What is this place?' She went over to the window and pressed her face against it. 'Nothing,' she said. 'There's nothing out there.'

'Nothing?' echoed Diana, coming up behind her.

'Zilch,' said Jenny. 'No reflection. You can usually see the street lights out there, right? And some bushes and stuff? But there's nothing. It's totally dark.'

'Perhaps it's a power cut,' Diana suggested. 'But then I suppose these lights wouldn't be on, would they?'

Jenny fiddled with the window catch. 'It won't open,' she said.

'All the windows have locks on them,' Diana explained. 'The key's . . .' She frowned. 'I can't remember where Oliver put the key. Let's try smashing it.'

Jenny looked doubtful. 'Are you *sure*?'

'It's not my window,' Diana said. 'I know it's not. And it's the only way we can find out what's out there.'

'I'm not so sure I want to find out,' Jenny said. But she slung the camera over her shoulder by its strap, leaving her hands free. She picked the ashtray up from the coffee table.

'Ready?' she asked. 'I guess I always wanted an excuse to smash a window. Here goes . . .' She swung her arm.

There was a thud. They examined the window. There was nothing, not even a crack. Jenny tried again, with no more success.

'Well, let's have one for the portrait album,' she said, taking aim at the room with her camera. 'Say cheese.'

Diana tried to duck out of the way, but the flash caught

107

her full in the face again. 'I don't want my photo taken here,' she said. 'It would be too . . . I don't know.'

'That reminds me . . .' Jenny felt in her pocket and drew out a crumpled square. She looked at it for a moment, and her face went white. 'Look,' she said, holding it out to Diana. 'The photo of the basement.'

Diana looked. 'Well,' she said doubtfully. 'It's us. And we're in the basement. There's you, and there's me, and there's the passageway.'

'Yeah,' said Jenny. 'But I *took* the photo, remember? *So how come I'm in it?*'

Diana stared at her. She looked back at the photo again. She snatched it from Jenny's hand and screwed it up.

'I don't think this is a dream,' she said in a small voice. 'But if it is, I *really* want to wake up.'

'It's not a dream,' Jenny said. 'It's real. But where are we? What the hell is this place?'

'It's like a photographic negative, everything the wrong way round,' Diana pointed to the magazine. 'Something that's being prepared, but which isn't quite ready yet. Perhaps it's all done with mirrors. Whoever put this room here hasn't quite got the hang of it yet. They need more practice. It's like a shell. It needs . . . finishing touches.'

Jenny shuddered visibly. 'What kind of finishing touches?'

Diana shook her head. 'Us . . .? No, that's too awful.'

The piano music tinkled to a halt. There was a pause, and then the voice of a radio announcer.

'. . . And now, Radio 3 is returning to the Orloff Institute for the second part of this afternoon's special broadcast: *The Underworld Tapes*, by Giuseppe Grosso. The first scene of the Third Act takes place in the princess's apartments, where she and her lady-in-waiting are being held prisoner by the mysterious man in grey . . .'

'Shit,' said Jenny. 'I'm gonna turn that thing off.'

She fiddled with the knobs on the radio. The volume increased.

'. . . the famous aria in which the princess muses upon her forthcoming marriage . . .'

'I see something!' Diana said, peering through the window. 'There's someone out there!'

Jenny had a feeling of foreboding, even before she turned towards the window. 'No, Diana!' she said. 'Don't look at it!'

But Diana was leaning forward, trying to get a better glimpse of the small, pale figure that was coming towards her through the darkness. It wasn't exactly walking. More like drifting across the ground. But there wasn't any ground, of course. Or if there was, it was too dark to see it.

'. . . and the little girl,' said the voice from the radio, 'is outside. She's hungry. She's cold. And she is waiting to come in . . .'

Jenny thumped the radio. She looked round. Diana was fiddling uselessly with the window catch.

The little girl hovered just outside the window so that her breath made condensation marks on the outside of the glass. She started to scratch at the pane with her fingernails. Her mouth opened. She was saying something, but they couldn't hear what it was.

'Diana,' said Jenny. 'That's the little girl from the dream. But there's something wrong with her. She looks different.'

'. . . Diana suddenly remembered,' the voice from the radio said, 'where the key was kept. It was behind the clock, of course. On the mantelpiece . . .'

'Of course!' Diana said triumphantly. She dived towards the clock and felt behind it. Her finger fastened round a small tube of metal.

'Diana! You can't let her in! Don't even *think* about it!'

'Shut up!' said the voice. Jenny stared at the radio in

disbelief. The voice continued in mellower tones, but faster, trying to ward off further intervention.

'Diana hurries to the window and opens it. The little girl, who is cold and hungry, is waiting to be let in. She falls gratefully into Diana's arms. . .'

'It's the little girl from the fairy-tale!' Diana exclaimed. She went back to the window, moving as if in a dream.

Jenny felt rooted to the spot. 'No!' she shouted. 'She's some sort of vampire, Diana. You mustn't let her in!'

The little girl's fingernails were scratching, scratching on the window.

'We can't leave her out there,' Diana said. 'She looks cold. And there are wolves in the forest.'

The little girl's eyes were pleading, beseeching. Jenny thought she saw something else there too. A gleam of malice, perhaps, tinged with an unearthly hunger.

'No, Diana!' she shouted. 'Look at her fingernails, for Christ's sake!'

Diana had inserted the key into the window lock. She paused and looked at the fingernails that were scrabbling on the pane. They were unnaturally long, and very dirty. Diana gasped. The key slipped out of her fingers and onto the ground.

The little girl's face creased up in an animal snarl. Her teeth, too, seemed longer, more pointed than they should have been.

'My God!' Diana said, taking a step backwards.

'. . . stupid, stupid Diana,' the radio announcer was saying, the voice working itself up into a high-pitched frenzy. 'If only she'd let the little girl in, then none of those awful things would have happened. But *oh no*, she had to behave like the stupid little twerp she was, had to listen to that lying American bitch . . .'

'Christ!' yelled Jenny. 'I've had enough of *you*, buddy!' She knocked the radio to the floor and stomped on it. The announcer began to babble, his voice rising to a screech. 'Stupid sluts! Strumpets! Stupid, stupid sluts! Slags! Bitches! Vile bitches!'

The little girl was still tapping at the window. Her face had changed back to its sweet, pleading self. Diana was caught in her gaze. She bent down to pick up the key.

'Filth!' shouted the announcer. 'Filthy whores!' Then Jenny brought her boot down. The radio exploded into pieces of wire and electronic shrapnel.

'Don't do it, Diana!' she said, but Diana didn't hear her. She was inserting the key into the window lock.

In desperation, Jenny brought the camera up and pressed the shutter. There was a blinding flash which seemed to last forever. It seared into her retinas and sent waves of dizzy heat through her brain.

Both girls reeled, blinking repeatedly. The room, and the little girl had gone. They were standing at the bottom of the basement steps. It was as though they had never been anywhere else.

Jenny stared at the picture that was developing in her hands. 'Christ!' she said. 'I'm getting *out* of this frigging place.' She hared up the steps and out into the hallway.

'Jenny! Wait!' Diana stumbled after her, still unable to see properly.

Jenny hesitated in the hallway. The door to Diana's flat stood slightly ajar. There was faint piano music coming from somewhere inside.

'Shit, no,' she said. 'I'm not going in *there*.' She thrust the camera at Diana. She screwed the Polaroid print into a small ball and hurled it to the floor behind her. She yanked the front door open and raced out into the street.

'Jenny!' Diana retrieved the crumpled print and tried to smooth it out. She could just about distinguish the side of her own head, vastly overexposed in the foreground. The blackness of the window loomed behind her, and in the window frame there was . . .

Jenny? No, it had to be a reflection. Jenny had taken the photo.

Diana didn't understand what she was seeing, but she didn't like it. She dropped the photo and pushed open her door.

It *was* her flat. There was no question about it. The mirror was its usual reflective self above the mantelpiece. Piano music was coming from the radio. She looked through the window. It was not yet dark. The flowerbed, the hedge and the street lights beyond it were clearly visible. She saw the top of a spiky blue-black head bobbing along as its owner ran down the road.

She threw the camera onto the sofa. Then picked up her keys and locked the door behind her.

She sprinted along the road. Jenny was already standing on the corner, waving her arms at every cab that went past.

'Jenny? Where are you going?'

Jenny shot her a look full of hurt and fury. 'Anywhere but here.'

Diana stuck out an arm. A vacant taxi pulled up beside them. Jenny clambered in. She said nothing as Diana climbed in after her.

And she said nothing as the cab wormed its way back into the line of traffic. It crawled, almost at a walking-pace, across town. Jenny's mouth was set in a grim line. She looked more frightened than anyone Diana had seen in her life.

*   *   *

Jenny collected her key from the desk and marched, tight-lipped, towards the lifts. Diana scampered after her, trying to keep up. The lift doors opened. They got in. Jenny was stony-faced and silent as they went up.

Diana couldn't stand it anymore. 'This is ridiculous,'

she said. 'You can't just run out on me like this. You can't run out on *yourself*. We've got to see this thing through.'

'It's *your* problem,' Jenny snapped. '*You* solve it. You can't drag *me* into it. It's nothing to do with *me*.'

The lift stopped. The doors slid open. Jenny struck out towards her room. She didn't seem to care whether Diana followed or not.

'Hey, wait a *minute*,' said Diana, feeling aggrieved. 'None of this started until I met *you* . . .'

Jenny unlocked her door and booted it open. Diana almost expected to have it slammed in her face. But Jenny ignored her. She marched straight across the room and began to pull things out of the wardrobe.

Diana crept in, shutting the door behind her. She perched on the edge of the bed and watched as a succession of T-shirts, socks and knickers flew across the room, landing in a heap on the floor.

'I guess you're thinking I'm to blame for all of this,' Jenny said at last. She stuffed a faded denim jacket into her holdall. 'Maybe you're thinking that it's me that's been giving you bad dreams.'

'No, I'm not,' Diana said. 'I was having nightmares before. It's just that they started to get worse as soon as you turned up on my doorstep. The trouble is, they don't seem like dreams any more. I can't tell when I'm awake and when I'm asleep.'

Jenny sat down on the bed next to Diana. She stared at the pile of clothes. 'I'm scared,' she said. 'That back-to-front apartment back there – was that a dream? That little girl at the window. Pardon my ignorance, Diana, but I had the impression we were both very much awake. I didn't see you dozing off on the sofa. We were both awake and we both *saw* it. It was *there*.'

'There must be an explanation,' Diana said. But if there was one, she couldn't think of it.

'I'll tell you what it is,' said Jenny. 'It's that Godawful freaking house. You're living in a crazy house, Diana. Shit, you couldn't get me back there if you paid me a million dollars.'

'You think it's haunted?'

'Well, it sure as hell isn't normal. I've got bad vibes about that place. I've had them all along. Maybe it's haunted, or maybe it's just us hallucinating. Maybe it *is* something to do with me. But there's something in the air there. And I don't like it.'

She picked up the phone and punched out a number on the buttons. 'Hi, Pan Am? I'd like to make a reservation to LA ... Now, today ... As soon as possible, then ... The name's Hoffman ... Okay, I'll be here for the next couple of hours.'

She gave the hotel's telephone number and slammed the receiver down. 'Looks like I'm stuck here until Wednesday at least.'

Diana studied her hands. She noticed that the nails, once so perfectly trimmed and polished, were now chewed to the quick. All those expensive manicures gone to waste.

Jenny's brusque manner softened a little. 'If I were you, I wouldn't go back there either,' she said. Now she seemed embarrassed. 'I'm sorry I ran out on you back there but, Jesus, I was scared shitless.'

'I've *got* to go back,' said Diana. 'What'll I say to Oliver? That there are little girls in the basement? That I'm having bad dreams? He knows about the dreams. I've told him, but he doesn't understand how bad they *are*.'

'Oh, *fuck* Oliver, said Jenny.

Diana was shocked.

'He wants to marry you, doesn't he?' Jenny went on. 'If he really loves you, he'll understand. He'll do whatever you ask.'

Diana wasn't so sure. 'It's not that he doesn't love me,'

she explained, trying to work it out for herself. 'It's just that everyone's gone to so much *trouble*. I can't just go to him and say "Hey, I've decided I don't want to live here after all".'

'Tell him you're allergic to the place,' said Jenny. 'Tell him . . . I don't know. Tell him it's overrun with cockroaches. Tell him people have *died* there. They have, you know. My folks did.'

'You think they're ghosts?'

Jenny shook her head. 'I guess not. Otherwise we'd have seen them. But that whole place is *weird*, you know. The way the basement changed like that.'

'It's like a dream factory,' Diana said.

'Sure,' said Jenny. 'Yeah. *Nightmares Are Us*. Shit, that's too much.'

She reached into a carrier bag by the bed and pulled out her bottle of vodka. 'Have a drink. Go on, Diana. You look like you need it.'

Diana hesitated. She wasn't keen on spirits. But she was cold and tired, very tired. And Jenny was holding the bottle out to her. She took what she hoped was a ladylike swig from it.

'God,' she said, wiping her mouth. 'I'm turning into an alcoholic.'

'No chance,' said Jenny, taking a much larger gulp herself. 'This is emergency rations. You've got a long way to go before total decadence sets in. Believe me.'

'Can I stay here for a while?' Diana asked. 'I don't want to go back, not just yet. Perhaps it *is* the house. I feel an awful lot better just being away from it.'

'Of course you can stay,' Jenny said. 'You can stay the night if you want. The bed's big enough. And I promise I won't make a pass at you.'

Diana forced a weak smile.

'Seriously though, Diana, you shouldn't go back on your own. Get Oliver or someone to go with you. You must *know* people.'

'Mmm,' said Diana. 'But it's Saturday. They'll all be out of town at the moment.' She stared at her hands again. 'Well, they might not *all* be away. But . . . they're not really . . . they're not the kind of people who . . .'

'Oh, I get it,' Jenny said. 'They get off on weddings and cocktail parties and all that shit. But they're not too keen on helping out when a girl's got problems.'

'That's about it,' Diana said sheepishly. 'They're nice people, they really are. But I can't talk to them like I can talk to you.'

Jenny looked flattered. 'Well, I guess that we've had fun together,' she said. 'That is, if you can overlook all the heebie-jeebie stuff.'

She took Diana's hand and squeezed it. 'You'll have to come over to LA when all this is over. I'll show you a good time, and no freaky business. I promise.'

She put the vodka down and stood up. 'If you like we can call room service and get something to eat.'

'Maybe later,' said Diana. She yawned. 'I'm so tired. I think I might lie down for a bit.'

'Oh Jesus,' Jenny said. 'Don't go to sleep, will you?'

'It's all right,' Diana murmured. 'We're not in the house, remember?' She stretched out on the bed.

'I guess it's okay. Go ahead. Get some sleep while you can. I'll keep an eye on you. I promise I'll wake you the minute you start twitching.'

Jenny went into the bathroom for a few minutes. By the time she came out, Diana was curled up on top of the orange bedspread. Her eyes were closed.

'Don't you *dare* dream,' said Jenny.

Diana murmured something under her breath. Jenny stood by the bed for a while, watching her carefully. Diana appeared to be sleeping peacefully at last. Her breathing was slow and even.

There was a sharp rap at the door. Jenny jumped.

She looked at Diana again. Diana didn't move. The noise hadn't got through to her.

'Who is it?' Jenny called in an undertone. She crossed to the door and put her ear against it.

'Room service.'

'I didn't order anything,' Jenny said. 'Not yet.' She looked at Diana. Diana was still sleeping soundly. She couldn't have started dreaming already. Not yet. And if she *were* dreaming, then surely it wouldn't be about anything so boring as room service.

'Well, somebody ordered it,' came the reply from the other side of the door. 'Chicken salad sandwiches. Coffee. Mineral water.'

'Somebody's made a mistake,' Jenny said. 'You'll have to take it back.'

'You gotta sign for it,' the voice pleaded. 'I don't care if you take it or not. You gotta sign, or I'll get into trouble.'

'Oh, bring it in then,' Jenny sighed. 'I'll take it. I was going to order something anyway.' She opened the door.

This turned out to be a big mistake. She realised that immediately, but it was too late. She tried to shut the door again, but a foot was thrust through the crack, wedging it open. She found herself looking into Paul Lawrence's face. He grinned humourlessly at her and pushed past into the room.

'Shit!' she said. 'I knew something fishy was going on. Get the fuck out of here.'

'Aw, c'mon,' he said, looking around him. 'You know you're pleased to see me. Don't pretend you're not.'

'Sure,' said Jenny. 'I'm wetting myself with delight. Now get out.' She held the door open for him. He made as if to go out, but grabbed it from her and slammed it shut instead.

'Now it's just the two of us,' he said. 'Us, and Sleeping Beauty here. Have I got news for *her*.'

'Leave her alone. Don't wake her up.'

Paul went over to the bed to look at the sleeping girl. 'What's with you two, anyway. You lesbians or something?'

'Fuck off,' said Jenny. 'She's had a rough time. She's tired. She needs rest.'

'What're you supposed to be?' sneered Paul. 'Her bodyguard? Don't tell me she's asked you to be her bridesmaid.'

'Look, say what you've got to say and scram.'

'Okay, okay,' said Paul, pretending to be hurt. 'I can see where I'm not wanted. I'm more sensitive than you think, you know.'

'Yeah, and I know *where* you're sensitive. And you'll be getting a boot there if you don't get out.'

'Only trying to help, darling. You do need help, don't you?'

Paul really did look a bit uncomfortable, Jenny realised. He really did look as though he would rather be somewhere else. The thought made her uneasy.

'I'm an investigative reporter, right? Well, tell your friend here that I've been doing some investigating. I've been digging into the files on her boyfriend, Mr High Flier. Old Joysticks.'

'So what?' snapped Jenny.

'He's in *big* trouble. He's practically borassic.'

'What?'

'Skint. Stony-broke. Out of brass. As good as bankrupt.'

'What's it got to do with you?' Jenny asked angrily. Her mind was racing.

'He's in *major debt.* Invested a packet in some Costa del Crime developments that went down the drain. Been trying to make up the loss ever since on the gaming tables. No dice, though. He's on a solid losing streak, and there are some pretty heavy characters twisting his arm. So, your little ladyfriend here: she isn't being led down the aisle. She's being led up the garden path. He doesn't want a wife; he wants a bleeding money bag.'

'Jesus!' said Jenny. 'What a slimeball.'

'She's not the only piece of skirt in his life, either. He's a right goer, that one.'

'Wait a bit,' said Jenny. 'You mean he's only marrying her for her money?'

'What else?' said Paul. 'You'll tell her, then? This is turning out to be some story. It'll make a great picture when she scratches his eyes out. Just make sure we get to know about it in advance. That's all I ask.'

Diana moaned softly. Jenny saw that her hands had bunched into tight fists. She moaned again, and kicked out at something in her sleep.

'Oh hell,' said Jenny. 'She's dreaming.' She made a move towards the bed, but Paul grabbed her arm.

'Tell me about it,' he said. 'Give me the inside story. What's been happening this last couple of days? How's he been treating her? Any hint that the hunk isn't all he's cracked up to be?'

Diana was writhing: curling and uncurling on the bed. She looked as though she'd been smitten by a severe stomach ache.

In her dream state, she realised that something was wrong. Horribly wrong. The two figures in her dream were talking about something she would rather not know, something too awful to contemplate. A fierce anger swept over her. She wanted the two figures to stop talking. She wanted them to go away.

Everything became clear for the first time. *She* was in control. She remembered someone talking to her in a dream. It's *you*, they had said. *You* did this. *She* had done it. *She* had made the photographer go away.

And now, there were these people standing over the bed, talking about things she didn't want to hear. She would make them go away too.

'Let go of me,' Jenny said. 'I've got to wake her up.'

'You just said she needed to sleep. What the hell's going on here anyway?'

'We can't let her dream,' Jenny said. Her knees suddenly buckled. There was a pounding behind her eyes. She felt a migraine coming on, and it was going to be a bad one. Her head felt like it was going to burst.

'God,' she said. 'I feel dizzy.'

'Take a nap, why don't you,' Paul sniggered. 'Don't let *me* stop you.'

'Diana!' she shouted. Diana's head turned towards the sound, but she didn't open her eyes. Her face was crinkled in concentration towards something that required her undivided attention.

'Look,' Jenny said, trying to pull away from Paul. 'She's dreaming about us. Don't you see? We've *got* to wake her up. Your photographer . . . Diana dreamt about *him*, and now he's disappeared . . .'

Paul whistled. 'So you *do* know something about it!' he said. 'You know what? I took the roll of film down the lab and had it developed. Do you know what was on it?'

'No,' said Jenny, still trying to tug away from him. 'Let me *go*! *Please*!'

'Pictures of your friend here,' Paul said. 'Giving Peck the old come-on, she was. Taking off her clothes, waving her knickers around. Posing in wet T-shirts. You think she's so bleeding refined. But she's not. She's a right little slut.'

Go *away*, Diana thought. She had to stop their stupid, wicked chatter. None of it was true. It couldn't possibly be true.

'But he's *gone*,' Jenny wailed. 'He fell down a hole in the basement. And then he tried to *kill* me.'

She managed to wriggle free of Paul at last. She staggered towards Diana, but her vision was blurring. There were two Dianas now. She reached out to wake one of them up.

And chose the wrong one. Her hand passed straight through Diana's shoulder.

Oh God, Jenny thought. It was too late. They were part of Diana's dream now.

'The basement? What the fuck are you talking about? Peck is . . .' Paul stopped talking and stared at his arms. Then he started to gabble. 'Fucking hell. What's happening to me? What the fuck's happening?'

Jenny looked at him helplessly. He was fading fast. The outline of the wardrobe was clearly visible through his body. His flesh was rippling, rearranging itself into another shape and receding into nothingness. He brought his hands up to his face. When he removed them, there was nothing there. What was left of him began to scream, even though he no longer had a mouth to scream with.

Whatever was happening to him, it was happening to Jenny too. She could see the pattern of the carpet through her hands. She felt herself being pulped by invisible fingers. They were squeezing the breath out of her, moulding her like putty.

Diana was doing it. She had to wake her up. It was their only chance.

Jenny stretched her arm out towards the sleeping girl, but she could no longer see where the arm ended and where the rest of the room began. And then she felt herself plucked into the air. The last gasp of breath rushed out of her lungs as she was smashed flat against the wall. She couldn't move. The wall was wrapping itself around her. She was melting *into* the wall.

Paul had stopped screaming. He was gone. There was only a smear like cold cream in the air where he'd been standing.

'Di . . . a . . . na . . .' Jenny tried to cry out, but her mouth had liquidised. It was running down her chin.

Diana thrashed around on the bed. She was in control, but something was going wrong. She had been tricked.

They had made her *think* she was in control, but *they* had tricked her. She was being manipulated. One of the figures had already gone, and the other was melting into the wall. She had to bring them back. Too late, she tried to undo what she had done.

She had to wake up.

Wake up, she thought. This was all a dream. This was not real. She *could* do it. She *could* wake up.

Her eyes were glued shut, like when she had had the measles. She applied concentrated willpower, tearing each eyelash free. Her eyelids were lined with sandpaper. She forced them up.

Her eyes were open.

But the nightmare didn't go away. She was in the hotel room and the wallpaper was moving. She could see the outline of a figure there; it looked as though it might once have been human. It was trapped like an insect on fly-paper, tearing itself to pieces in an effort to escape.

The figure was becoming less distinct by the second.

'Di . . . a . . . naaaa . . .'

Diana sat up. She thought she could hear Jenny's voice, calling her from a long way off. Just for a second, she thought she could see the outline of a face against the wall. But then, with a last despairing wail, the face was gone.

Diana leapt to her feet and hurled herself at the wall, hammering on it with her fists. It was as solid as she was. She thought that perhaps there was some sort of after-image on the wallpaper, a fading stain.

And then, that too was gone. She wasn't so sure that it had ever been there.

She was alone in the hotel room.

Jenny's bag lay half-packed on the floor. Diana opened the bathroom door. Jenny was nowhere to be seen.

The telephone buzzed. Diana lifted the receiver numbly.

'Miss Hoffman? About your flight reservation . . . We happen to have a cancellation for tomorrow morning . . .'

'No . . .' said Diana. 'I'm sorry, but Miss Hoffman's not here right now. I'll get her to call you when she gets back . . .' She replaced the receiver.

What was going on? Where *was* Jenny? Had Diana really dreamt her away? Where *was* she? Diana let out a cry of rage and frustration. It wasn't the house that was giving her bad dreams at all, then. It was *her*. It was all *her*. Whatever had been at the house, it had become a part of her. And now it was here, in the hotel.

She told herself to keep calm. She wouldn't lose her head. That was what *they* wanted. Well, she wouldn't be giving them that satisfaction. Jenny had popped out. She'd be back in a minute. She would.

Diana crossed to the door and opened it cautiously, not knowing what to expect. A maid trundled a trolley heaped with bed linen along the hotel corridor. A door slammed, and an elderly couple hobbled off towards the lifts. From somewhere there came the distant hum of a vacuum-cleaner.

Diana pulled the door to and set off down the corridor. There was no sign of the elderly couple by the time she reached the lifts. She pressed the down arrow. The door slid back immediately. She stepped inside and pushed the button marked 'lobby'. The door slid shut. The lift began to move downwards.

If Jenny wasn't to be found, she decided, she would go and see Deborah. She didn't want to go back to the flat. Not just yet. She would see Deborah and tell her what had happened. Deborah would understand.

The lift shuddered to a halt and the door slid open.

'Oh *no!*' Diana groaned as she saw what lay in front of her. 'No, no *no!*'

There was no lobby. There was no longer any hotel, only the hotel lift. The art deco light fittings on either side of it cast a warm orange glow onto the walls of the brick-lined passageway. It stretched as far as the eye could see in either direction, disappearing into distant shadow.

There was a faint sound. The steady slap of running feet, drawing closer, getting louder all the time.

A long way down the passageway, a figure broke free of the shadows. It was running towards her. Running hard.

Panicked, Diana slammed her hand down on the lift controls. The door slid shut. The lift didn't move.

Move, damn you. She slammed her hand down on the buttons again.

The lift stayed where it was. The door slid open. The figure was still running along the passageway towards her. The figure was getting closer.

The figure was there. It was Paul Lawrence. He was out of breath. He looked bewildered. A little scared, even. She had the fleeting impression that he was running away from someone. Or something.

He flung himself into the lift beside her. 'What the hell's going on?' he demanded. He started to pound on the controls. 'Come on, sister, *move it!*'

The door slid shut. The lift started to move. With dawning horror, Diana realised they were going down. It was impossible. The button for the lobby was the last one. There was nowhere to go down *to*. In the overhead light, Paul's face seemed full of shadows.

'Where is she? Where's Jenny?' asked Diana.

'Where is *she*?' echoed Paul. 'Who gives a toss where *she* is? Where are *we*? That's what *I* want to know.'

For an instant, Diana thought she'd been mistaken. It wasn't Paul Lawrence at all. His nose was too hooked. His mouth was far too wide. His lips curled back to reveal teeth much longer and sharper than she remembered Paul Lawrence having.

But it *was* Paul Lawrence. 'You *got* me here,' he said petulantly. 'Now *you* get me back, or else. Dream me back, bitch. *I don't like it here.*'

He suddenly seemed much taller. He loomed over her. Diana pressed herself back into the corner of the lift. She noticed with disgust that his fingernails were dirty. And extremely long.

'I don't like it down here,' he said again. This time his tone was more threatening. '*You don't know what they're trying to turn me into.*'

The lift moved slowly downwards. Diana tried not to panic. She forced herself to think.

She willed the lift to come to a stop. It did. With an effort that made stars explode behind her eyes, she made the door slide open.

Paul Lawrence was caught off guard. He looked round, surprised. Diana ducked under his arm and ran out.

She had to bite her lip to prevent herself crying out. She was back in the basement. There was no escaping from it.

'Hey!' the journalist shouted behind her. 'You don't want to go out there! Come back!' He started after her.

There was no choice but to follow the passageway. A little further on there was a sharp twist, and the path branched out in all directions. She had the feeling it wouldn't matter which route she chose. They would all lead to the same thing. The basement had already decided where it was taking her.

It took her straight into the arms of the fat man. He was waiting for her. His bulk blocked the passageway. There was no way past.

She skidded to a halt, just managing to stop herself from cannoning into him. He had changed since she had last seen him. Where had that been? In a dream? In real life? She couldn't be sure any more. He was fatter than ever. He was gross, obese. The filthy jacket was stretched tight over his enormous bulging girth. His skin, too, looked as if it had been stretched over something that was straining to get out. His trousers were dappled with dark stains. He looked as though he had been eating. There were brown encrustations on the front of his shirt and chin. A few wormlike noodles still clung to the corner of his mouth.

'Hello, darling,' he said. It looked and sounded as though his mouth was still full of half-masticated food. A few more wormy tendrils snaked free as he spoke.

She started to back away, but it was useless. Paul came up behind her.

'Hello, Paulie!' Peck chuckled gleefully at the sight of him. 'You down here too? What took you so long?'

'You've been feeding your fat face again,' Paul said. 'Too much junk food, my old son. Look where it's got you.'

He shook with laughter. Peck joined in, snorting like a pig. 'Good nosh down here,' he slobbered. 'You'll like it. Bring your ladyfriend: she looks like a bit of all right. We can make up a threesome.' He made an obscene gesture with his fingers and creased up with laughter. A thin noodle slithered out of his nostril and hung, quivering, over his lip.

Diana stared at it in revulsion. Something snapped inside her. She felt blind anger welling up. How *dare* they do this to her? Who did they think they were?

'Stop it!' she shouted. 'Stop it! You're disgusting! Both of you!'

She lashed out without thinking. Her fist connected with Peck's face. There was an explosion of rotting meat as his flesh collapsed like an overripe fruit, spraying her with pus and blood.

'Wow,' said Paul, deeply impressed.

Diana stared at her hand. It was dripping with a glutinous orange liquid. The stench hit the back of her sinuses and lodged there. She felt sick. It smelt like sweet-and-sour sauce.

Peck's massive body was rocking on its heels. Brown mucus was still oozing out of the hole in the ruined head. There were wormy bits in it, and small chunks of solid matter. It looked as though someone had punched a carton of Chinese food.

'Oooh,' said Paul. 'You've been a very naughty girl. Look what you've done.'

He seized Diana by the shoulder and shook her till the teeth rattled in her head. She decided it was time to scream.

He had her by the shoulders. He was shaking her roughly, backwards and forwards. Her teeth were rattling. Her head snapped back. She thought it was going to fall off.

'*Diana! Wake up!*'

She forced her eyes open. She saw a face hovering anxiously over her. The face was attached, very definitely, to a body. It was Jenny.

'Jenny?' She reached out and touched Jenny's arm. The American girl was solid, *all there*.

'Jenny! What . . .'

'You were dreaming,' said Jenny. 'It looked bad. You were shouting in your sleep. Screaming. But I managed to wake you before anything happened. Are you okay?'

'I think so,' Diana said. She sat up.

All at once she knew she was going to be sick. She just made it into the bathroom in time.

Jenny heard the sounds of retching, then the noise of running water as Diana rinsed her hand under the tap again and again. She staggered back to the bed, her face still grey.

'*That* bad, huh?'

She held out the bottle of vodka, but Diana shook her head.

'I dreamt . . . I dreamt . . .'

'No, don't tell me. I don't think I want to know.'

'But I dreamt you disappeared . . .'

'Well, I'm still here,' said Jenny. 'Whatever you were dreaming about, it didn't affect me this time. It must have been just a normal, everyday, pretty revolting nightmare.'

'How long was I asleep?'

Jenny shrugged. 'Not long. Ten minutes, maybe.'

'The reporter, Paul Lawrence. Was he here?'

'Paul Lawrence? Oh, you mean the scumbag. No, of course he wasn't. He can't find us, Diana. There's no way he could have followed us here. We only had one visitor, and that was room service.' She pointed over to a small pile of sandwiches on a tray. There was coffee there too, and a bottle of Perrier. 'Hungry? You want some?'

Diana felt her stomach heave at the sight of the food. 'No. Nothing to eat. Not just now. Perhaps I should have some coffee, though. Perhaps that'll make me feel more awake.'

She suddenly remembered something. 'Your flight. To Los Angeles. The airline called. I answered the phone . . .'

'Nah,' said Jenny, shaking her head. '*I* answered the phone. You must have heard it and somehow incorporated it into your dream. There was a seat on tomorrow's flight. I . . . decided not to take it. Looks like I'm stuck here for another three days, at least.'

'I'm glad you're not going back just yet,' Diana said.

'Yeah,' said Jenny. 'I couldn't *really* have run out on you, you know. I just freaked out after all that weird shit back at the apartment.'

'We have to go back there, sooner or later.'

'Better make that later. *Much* later. Like *never*.'

'It's the only way,' Diana insisted. 'Really it is. And look, it's not the same now. I think I've discovered something. This thing works both ways. *They* can get at us, but *we* can get back at them. Listen . . .'

She told Jenny about the dream. She skimmed over the part about Jenny and Paul Lawrence disappearing; she didn't want to get her spooked again. But she described the scene in the lift, and how she'd managed to get the doors open.

'Yeah, that's pretty neat,' Jenny said, impressed. 'What happened then?'

Diana told her about Peck exploding into mush.

'*Yuck*!' said Jenny, making a face. 'No wonder you threw up.'

'What do you think?' Diana asked. 'Do you think I can change what happens in the dreams?'

Jenny didn't look too hopeful. 'If you *are* in control, how come you didn't manage to wake yourself up when it got bad?' she asked.

'I don't know,' Diana said. 'Perhaps I just need more practice.'

Jenny wasn't convinced. 'Opening elevator doors is one thing,' she said. 'Coping with those psycho creeps is another. What we need is drugs. Speed or something. So we can keep you awake till we work out what's going on.'

'Drugs?' Diana said. 'Where would we get drugs from?'

Jenny shrugged. 'I haven't got a clue. I'd know where to go in LA. But London . . . I guess we'll have to forget the idea. Unless any of your society friends happen to be closet cokeheads.'

Diana remembered what Deborah had said. 'Deborah might be able to help,' she suggested. 'She said she could give me something if the dreams got really bad.'

'Your friend the shrink!' Jenny snapped her fingers. 'Of course! Where do we reach her?'

Diana made some phone calls and finally tracked Deborah down. She was still at the clinic. She sounded concerned as Diana explained, hesitantly, what she wanted.

'Amphetamine is the last thing you want,' she said. 'What you need is a good night's sleep. You sound dreadful. Look, let's meet anyway. Why don't you both come on over? I've finished for the evening. We can talk. Try and work out what's best.'

'All right,' said Diana. 'We're on our way.'

She force-fed herself on black coffee. Then she rooted through Jenny's make-up bag, trying to find something to put colour into her cheeks. She smoothed on some blusher.

'That's no good,' she said, staring at her reflection. 'It's grotesque. I look like Coco the Clown.'

'Hmmm,' said Jenny. 'You look fine.'

'Liar,' said Diana. She wiped her face clean again.

'Yeah,' said Jenny. 'You *do* look better without. Pale but interesting. Are you ready to rock?'

'Uh-huh,' Diana replied. 'Let's go.'

Jenny locked up. They set off down the corridor.

'Now, tell me,' said Diana. 'I am awake, aren't I?'

'I sure hope so,' Jenny replied. 'If you're not, then you're making a pretty good job of pretending to be. Walking and talking and so on.'

'I just get confused.'

'*You're* confused? How do you think *I* feel? You know, maybe it's that Zen thing. Maybe all our lives are just part of someone else's dream. Maybe none of us is real. When they wake up – zap! – we vanish!'

'Don't,' said Diana, shivering. 'That's too horrible.'

They reached the lifts. Jenny pressed the call button. Diana stared hard at the doors. They slid open. She stepped back.

'No,' she said. 'I'm not getting in the lift. I know where it goes.'

'Okay,' said Jenny. 'No problem. We'll take the

stairs.' Diana followed her across the hallway to the door marked Emergency Exit. They pushed it open and went through.

Whoever had decorated the hotel had obviously decided that the stairway wasn't going to be in regular use. Nobody had bothered to make it look in the least bit luxurious. It was clean – there was a faint smell of disinfectant – but there was no deep-pile carpet or plush wallpaper. There weren't even any windows. Bare stone steps led up and down, lit by bare bulbs that looked as though they were on permanent emergency power.

They started walking down.

They'd got as far as the third floor when there was a metallic clanging from somewhere above them.

Jenny stopped. 'Sssh,' she said. 'Did you hear that?'

Diana had heard it. She didn't stop. It sounded as though someone had pushed through the doors a few floors above. The hollow clack of descending footsteps echoed down.

Diana and Jenny exchanged glances. Both of them felt a nameless dread. They walked faster.

Diana panicked. The footsteps were getting closer. She didn't know who was behind them, but she certainly didn't feel like finding out. They reached the second floor. There was a door there. She dived towards it and fell against the metal bar.

'In here!' she hissed at Jenny. 'Quick!' The bar gave way beneath her weight. The door opened inwards. She tumbled through.

Jenny tried to follow her. The door swung shut in her face. She shoved at the bar. Nothing happened. It wouldn't move.

'Diana!' she shouted. 'Open the door! I can't get in!' She hammered frantically on the glass panel.

Diana heard her, and turned. She pushed and pulled at the inside of the door. It wouldn't budge. Jenny's face was pressed up against the glass. The lights on the stairway were going out behind her, one by one.

Diana pushed at the door again. It still wouldn't move. 'Jenny!' she yelled. 'Go down to the next floor! *The next floor down*! I'll meet you there!'

Jenny didn't appear to have heard. Diana saw her glance briefly over her shoulder. When she turned round again, her face was as pale as a ghost's.

'*Diana!*' she called. Her voice was muffled.

Then, as Diana watched, the darkness enveloped her and she was gone. Swallowed up.

Diana summoned all her strength for one last shove at the door. It swung open easily. The lights flickered and came on. There was no one there. The stairway was completely deserted.

Diana fell back and let the door swing shut. She sank to the floor, exhausted. They were playing some sort of sadistic game. Some sort of ghoulish hide and seek. They wanted her to join in? She'd play. All right, she *had* to play. But she wished they'd stop changing the rules. It wasn't fair. Everyone was ganging up against her. They were all huddled together somewhere, like sardines, giggling. Everyone was in on the joke. Except her.

What was she supposed to do now? Search for Jenny? Go back to the flat? Find Deborah? All she wanted to do was to go to sleep.

But, if this was a dream, then she was asleep already.

And if it wasn't a dream . . .? If it was *real*?

She looked around her. The corridor seemed real enough, but it looked as though the decorators had slipped up again. This part of the hotel was older, dustier than the other floors. The wallpaper was brown, the carpet threadbare. Diana began to wonder whether she was in the hotel at all. Wearily, she got to her feet and began to walk. She had no idea where she was going.

'. . . And you'll do as I say!' A man backed out of a

doorway some yards ahead of her. 'I don't want to hear any more nonsense about this so-called friend of yours!'

He was wearing a paint-spattered overall. One of the decorators, Diana thought.

But no. He pulled someone out of the doorway after him. It was a little girl.

Diana recognised her instantly. It was the little girl who had scratched at the window, the little girl from the book of fairy-tales. Horrible little beast, Diana thought. It served her right. But then she felt guilty. The little girl was squealing in terror. The man had her by the arm. He was dragging her across the floor.

'It wasn't me!' she cried. 'It wasn't me! It was Angela!'

Diana pressed herself against the wall, but neither the man nor the little girl had seen her. The man picked the child up and tucked her easily under his arm. He strode down the corridor, away from Diana. The little girl kicked and screamed, but he took no notice.

Diana followed them down the corridor, keeping her distance. The doors that she passed had no numbers on them. They were locked, and she had no desire to find out what lay on the other side. The place appeared to be deserted, apart from the three of them. The man swung to his right and disappeared. Diana saw the top of a staircase. Now she *knew* they were no longer in the hotel.

She leaned over the bannisters and saw the top of the man's head bobbing as he descended. Diana lost sight of them as they reached the bottom of the steps, but she could still hear their voices.

'I want my mummy!' the child wailed.

'Well, you can't *have* your mummy!' shouted the man. 'You know why, don't you, you little brat? You can't have her because she's *dead*! And you know why she's dead, don't you?'

'Nooo! I don't want to go down there!' screamed the little girl. 'You can't make me!'

Diana had got halfway down the stairs when she realised with a shock where they were. Below her, there was carpet where there should have been chequered tiling. The place was in shadow, but she could see that the walls were brown where they should have been white. It all looked very different, but she knew exactly where she was. She was in the hallway of her own house.

There was no time to stop and think about how they'd got there. The little girl was sobbing now. She sounded terrified. Diana decided she would have to intervene. She reached the bottom of the steps.

She couldn't see the man, but she could hear him yelling: 'She's dead because you *killed* her!'

Diana looked across the hallway. It was *her* hallway, but there was no familiar doorway leading to her flat. The wall was unbroken except for a small oil painting of a gloomy landscape.

The door was in the wrong place. It was further back. It was open.

The voices changed. The man was muttering in a low voice, saying something she couldn't hear clearly. The little girl was laughing. No, not laughing. She was sobbing uncontrollably.

Diana took a few steps towards the door. There was a sudden *whoosh* ahead of her and the hallway was bathed in flickering orange light. She jumped back, startled.

Someone was screaming. At first, she thought it was the little girl. Then she realised it was the man's voice. She crept forward again.

The screaming had gone up an octave. Now it hardly sounded human. Diana covered her ears with her hands, but the sound still pierced her eardrums.

The man danced out of the room towards her, trailing flame. He twirled and flapped his arms like a flightless bird trying to take off. He was blazing like a torch. Diana felt a gust of searing heat as he lurched past her, and then he was off down the hallway, stumbling against the walls, leaving them blackened and smoking.

The door to the basement was open. The man spun round once, then hurled himself through it. The screaming was abruptly cut off. Diana heard the heavy crash of a body, bumping and rolling down the basement steps.

She turned back to the room and peered inside. The room was ablaze. It was full of grotesque figures, all of them writhing in the grip of the flames. Diana realised with relief that they weren't real people at all: they were statues and carvings. The one burning brightest appeared to be made of wood, tree people with crackling limbs. Other forms were melting in the heat, their noses and eyes merging into liquid streams, arms reduced to softened stumps.

In the centre of the room was an elaborate still life. It reminded Diana of the Christmas grotto she had once visited with her nanny. It was arranged to resemble a woodland glade, littered with dried leaves and the branches of trees, populated by small stuffed animals.

The little girl was sitting on a tree trunk. There was a stuffed rabbit on her lap. She was talking to it, stroking its ears. She didn't appear to have noticed the flames that were now licking at the edges of the glade. The leaves crackled as they caught fire.

Diana barely hesitated. Dream or no dream, she couldn't leave the little girl there to burn to death. She wove her way towards the tree, dodging the flames and trying not to breathe the smoke.

The little girl looked up and saw her. 'Hello,' she said. 'My name's Angela. What's yours?'

Diana tried to answer, but the smoke got into her mouth and made her cough and splutter. The little girl smiled at her, looking for all the world as though she spent her life sitting around in blazing rooms. Diana bent down and scooped the little girl into her arms. The rabbit fell into the flames.

The smoke was so thick now that Diana could hardly see the door. The heat was blistering. There was a smell of singed hair. All those hours at the hairdresser's, she thought, all down the drain. Behind them, one of the trees toppled over with a crash.

Just as she thought they would never make it, they reached the doorway. It was edged in flame, like a blazing gate to hell. The fire flared up as they passed through it. And then, just as suddenly, dwindled. The room faded into blackness behind them, a smoking shell.

Diana stepped out into the hallway and into the teeth of an Arctic gale. The wind almost swept off her feet. Freezing snow whipped into her face. She had plunged from the inferno into sub-zero temperatures. *Got too hot for you?* she thought grimly. *Well, let's cool off a little.*

Still clutching the little girl, she edged forward, trying to keep her footing in the patches of ice that were forming on the ground.

She could hardly see where she was going. Her eye-lashes were clogging up with snowflakes, but she sensed that the hallway had changed again. The walls had expanded outwards. She was toiling across a vast white landscape, towards the bottom of some steps.

The cold wormed its way through her thin clothes and bit into her flesh. Her teeth began to chatter like castanets. She felt light-headed. Only a few moments ago she'd almost been roasted, and now here she was, in danger of freezing to death.

She reached the steps and started to drag herself up them. The little girl's body was like a lump of ice in her arms. Just a bit further, Diana kept saying to herself. A few steps more. Just a bit further.

Their path was blocked by a door. Diana fumbled for the knob with fingers turned blue and numb. The door opened.

The wind swept her through. She leant back on the

door to force it shut. The blizzard was instantly cut off.

Diana stared in confusion. She was back in the hallway. She had come up from the basement. But . . . she thought, and gave up. There was no point in trying to work it out now.

She pulled the keys from her pocket and unlocked the door to her flat. The small body seemed to be getting heavier by the minute. She carried it into her bedroom and laid it down on the bed.

The little girl's face was coated with a thick layer of frost. Diana couldn't even see if she was breathing. She took one of the small hands in her own, rubbing it to try and bring the warmth back. There was the faintest suggestion of a pulse fluttering weakly in the wrist. Diana decided that she would have to get help, and quickly, or the child might die of exposure.

She was about to pick up the phone when it rang. She snatched up the receiver, not knowing what to expect.

'Hello sweetheart,' said Oliver. 'It's me.'

The sound of his voice wasn't as reassuring as it should have been. What was it she'd been trying to remember about him? She shook herself free of the dark thoughts that crowded in on her brain. There were more urgent things to worry about now.

'Oliver!' she gasped. 'I need your help. You've got to get over here right away.'

'What's up, darling? You sound out of breath.'

'It's a matter of life and death,' Diana said. 'There's been some sort of accident. There's a little girl here. She needs help.'

'Good God, Diana! What's going on? Are you all right? Shall I phone for an ambulance?'

'No!' said Diana. 'No ambulance! Just you, Oliver. *Please*. I need you. Quickly!'

'Okay, darling, okay.' Oliver sounded weary. 'I'll be right there. Give me ten minutes.'

He hung up, and she was left wondering where he'd been calling from. He was supposed to be at the base, but if it was only going to take him ten minutes to get here . . .

But there was no time for that now. The frost was disappearing from the little girl's face. Melted ice trickled down and left damp marks on the pillow.

Diana gazed at the small face. The little girl couldn't possibly be a phantom. She was real. Solid. She had certainly been heavy enough when Diana was carrying her up the stairs.

This was not the same little girl as the one at the window, she decided. They looked alike, but this one was a real, sweet, innocent little girl. Perhaps they were twins. This one's fingernails were little-girl length. She opened her eyes, and they were little-girl eyes. They stared out at Diana in pain and bewilderment. The little face crumpled, but it was not into an animal snarl. She started to sob.

'You poor little thing,' said Diana, stroking damp hair back from the forehead. 'It's all right now.'

The little girl whispered something.

'Yes, lovey, what is it?' Diana bent closer to hear what she was saying.

'Diana . . .' whispered the little girl.

How does she know my name? thought Diana, as the little girl raised thin arms and buried her face in Diana's neck.

Diana's skin crawled at the little girl's touch. The little girl's hands were colder than the ice that had melted from her face. They were cold and clammy.

Diana tried to pull away, but the little girl clung on tighter. She seemed suddenly to have put on a great deal of weight. There was no getting round the fact: she was not a little girl any longer.

'Helloooo,' said the voice, in falsetto.

The face came up then, and Diana saw who it was.

138

Peck's head had reconstituted itself. But whoever had put it back together again had got things wrong. The nose was where the mouth should have been, and the mouth . . .

He wrapped his arms around her. She tried to scream, but something slithered into her gullet and almost choked her. Her mouth was full of congealed noodles. Her nostrils were clogged with the smell of chop suey. Her stomach heaved. She realised that, no matter what happened, she would never again be able to look at a bowl of Chinese food.

This wasn't really happening, she told herself. This was all a dream. And it was *her* dream. She was going to take control of it. She was going to wake herself up. Now.

She closed her eyes as tight as she could. Even as she did so, she knew it was no use. She would have to face facts. They'd got her exactly where they wanted her. She wasn't in control; *they were*. She opened her eyes.

'Wakey, wakey!' cooed Peck. He licked his lips with what should have been his tongue, but she wasn't sure. It was difficult to tell.

There was one chance. She had smashed his head to mush before. She could do it again.

'Go . . . away . . .' she managed to croak. She lashed out with all the strength she could muster. Her hand connected with something soft, and sank in.

'Ooof!' Peck's arms fell away from her.

'Go away!' she repeated, feeling stronger now. 'Leave me alone, you fucking creep!'

'*Diana!*'

The voice was no longer Peck's voice. She had thought that her eyes were already open, but they weren't. She opened them now.

There were two faces bent over her, both of them tense with shock. Oliver and Deborah. Oliver was cradling his chin as though he had toothache.

'Oh, Oliver!' she gasped. 'Deborah! I'm so glad to see you!'

She burst into tears. They watched silently as she snivelled. Deborah handed her a paper tissue and she blew her nose into it noisily.

'What on earth's going on?' asked Oliver. 'Diana, you look dreadful. What have you done to yourself, darling? Where's this little girl you were talking about?'

'It wasn't a little girl at all,' Diana snuffled. 'The room was on fire, there was a man, he burned to death, but I saved her, and then there was a snowstorm, but it wasn't her at all, it was the fat man and I think they're some sort of dream spirits, they want me, they want me but they're not going to get me, I won't let them, I have control of my dreams now, I woke myself up, didn't I? They want Jenny too, they've had her before, but she escaped, but they want her now, for keeps . . .'

Oliver and Deborah exchanged glances. Diana caught sight of their faces and shut herself up. She was babbling. She knew she was. They must be thinking she was bonkers.

'And where *is* Jenny?' Deborah asked. She leant over Diana and picked up her wrist. Then she unbuttoned the cuff of her blouse and rolled the sleeve, smeared with soot and grime, up past Diana's elbow.

Diana suddenly thought about Jenny. 'Oh my God, she's trapped. We've got to help her.' She tried to get up, but fell back on the bed, exhausted. Deborah bent down and drew a syringe from her case.

'Trapped where?' asked Deborah.

She's humouring me, Diana thought. Deborah was just like the rest of them. They were all in it together.

'In the dream . . .' she said limply. It didn't sound too good. She knew it didn't. She couldn't blame them for not believing, not really. But she did blame them for not understanding, for not even *trying* to help.

She didn't want to talk to Deborah any more. She wanted to talk to Jenny. Jenny was the only one who would understand.

But Jenny was gone.

'Oh, for . . .' Oliver opened his mouth to say something. He saw a warning in Deborah's eye and thought better of it. He was gazing at the floor, Diana saw, as though he were embarrassed.

'Listen to me, Diana,' Deborah said in a sing-song voice. She sounded as though she were addressing a small child. 'I'm giving you something to make you relax. Now don't worry; this will be a dreamless sleep. There will be no more nightmares. We can work everything out when you wake up. Everything's going to be fine . . .'

She slid the needle into Diana's arm.

'No!' said Diana, trying to pull away. 'I've got to go back in and get her, don't you see? She's trapped there . . .'

The room, and Deborah and Oliver with it, was receding into the distance. A feeling of warmth and well-being flooded through her. She welcomed it, even though the feeling was tinged with guilt. Jenny needed her help. She should be looking for Jenny.

Jenny would have to wait.

Dreamless sleep. It seemed too good to be true.

Oliver's voice drifted towards her through time and space. 'What's going on? Is she having a breakdown?'

Thanks, Oliver, she thought. Thanks a million. A breakdown. That was all she needed.

Then the warm, velvety darkness opened up and she sank into it.

SATURDAY

Diana swam. She saw the surface gleaming like a flat green mirror above her. She struck out towards it, gliding easily through the water. It was cool down here, and comfortable. She felt like staying for ever.

But she knew it was important to get to the surface. She couldn't remember why. It just was. They *wanted* her to stay down here. Whoever they were.

Bubbles drifted past her head. She eyed them as she swam. It was like being trapped in a bottle of Perrier. She swam faster. The bubbles rushed past her. Her lungs felt as if they were about to burst.

She sucked in a great gasp of air, and surfaced in a small room. She blinked. Once. Twice. It wasn't her room. She was lying in a bed. It wasn't her bed. She was tucked in so tightly that she could barely move her legs.

She saw tiny pieces of sticking plaster attached to the inside of her arms. Something was pulling at the skin on her forehead. She wrinkled it. There were two more pieces of plaster there; she could feel them. She raised her head. There were other pieces on her chest, she saw, under the white cotton nightgown. It wasn't her nightgown.

Each piece of plaster was attached to a length of wire. Each wire disappeared into a thin plastic tube. She followed the tubes with her eyes. They wound away to a metal trolley on her left. There was a bank of machinery on the trolley. Small green lights winked and flickered.

It reminded her of the stereo amplifier which Oliver had set up in the flat. She could hear a faint bleeping noise. It seemed to be coming from one of the machines.

She didn't feel like getting up. The effort of looking round the room had exhausted her. She closed her eyes and tried to drift back down into the deep green place that had been so comfortable.

There was the sound of a door opening, and footsteps. She peeked through her eyelashes. Deborah was walking towards the bed. Oliver trailed after her.

Diana's mind was foggy. She didn't feel like talking to either of them. Anyway, they didn't understand. They thought she'd gone mad. Perhaps she *had* gone mad. That would be the easiest explanation.

'I don't see what good I can do here,' Oliver was saying. 'Look, why don't you call her parents? I have to get back to base.'

'Don't try it on with me,' Deborah said. There was a flinty edge to her voice that Diana had never heard before. 'Both you and I know that you have absolutely no intention of going back to base. Who is it now, Oliver? That blonde bint I saw you with at the Claremont? Or maybe you're still tooling around with the Swedish tart?'

Diana wondered what she was talking about. She kept her eyes closed. She resisted the pull of the green ocean, and tried to concentrate on what Deborah and Oliver were saying.

'Keep your mouth shut,' Oliver said. 'You wouldn't want me talking to the press about that methadone business, would you? You'd be struck off, and you know it. You'd never be allowed to work with children again. You'd never be allowed to work with *anyone* again. The wedding will go ahead as planned and that's that.'

'Oh yes, the wedding,' Deborah said. 'Don't you think the wedding should be postponed for a while? Until Diana is fit and well?'

'My dear Deborah, I have my doubts that little Diana will *ever* be fit and well. Anyway, we've made all the arrangements, sent out all the invitations. It's too late to back out now, even if it does mean I end up married to a lunatic.'

Diana felt curiously detached from what she was hearing. They couldn't possibly be talking about *her*. They had to be talking about someone else. Why was Oliver saying these things? He sounded so smooth, so confident. But was she imagining it, or was there a hint of panic in his voice? He was worried about her. She knew he was.

'Come on, Debs,' he was saying. 'For old time's sake . . .'

'*What* old times, Diana thought. Then she remembered. It was Deborah who'd first introduced her to Oliver. Of course. They were old friends.

Perhaps, she thought, they'd been more than old friends.

'I know what you're up to,' Deborah said. 'And I don't like it. You can treat me like dirt, if you like, and any of the others. I knew what I was getting myself into. But Diana's different. She adores you, don't you realise? She's still a child. You've no right to do this to her.'

'Do *what*?' Oliver snapped. 'It's *your* fault. You've been putting all this nonsense into her head from the beginning. All this nightmare mumbo-jumbo. Because you're jealous. You can't bear the thought of me marrying her. And you'd be only too happy to get your hooks into her, wouldn't you? Markham would throw money at you if he thought it would make his darling daughter well again. Think of it, Deborah. Private funding for your precious dream research.'

Diana was amazed. Without thinking, she opened her mouth to say something. She caught herself just in time. She turned the sound into a mumble, shifting on her pillow in what she hoped was a credible simulation of sleep.

'She's coming round,' said Deborah. 'You'd better decide what you're going to do. But remember this: the wedding's off. Whether it'll ever be on again is entirely up to you.'

'Bitch,' Oliver said evenly. 'I'm not hanging around here to watch you stick needles in the kid. You may not believe this, but at least I respect Diana as a person. I don't like to see her like this, being used as some sort of glorified guinea-pig.'

There was an awkward pause, then Oliver's voice rose again. 'Look, I really do hope she gets better. I'll drop by tomorrow. Maybe we can get some sense out of her then.'

Footsteps. The door slammed. Diana opened her eyes.

Deborah was gazing down at her. 'Sssh,' she said. 'It's all right. He's gone now.'

Diana felt a small pinprick on the inside of her arm. She closed her eyes again; she didn't want to see the blood that would well up and stain her wedding dress. She sank gratefully back into the dim coolness of the big green pool and floated there lazily.

Once or twice, she felt a small ripple sweeping through the calm, buffeting her gently. Once, she thought she could hear a small voice as it carried towards her on the current.

'Diana!' it cried from somewhere a long way off. 'Help me!'

'Jenny,' she murmured drowsily. 'Hold on, Jenny. I'm coming.'

But not yet. Not just yet . . .

*   *   *

Jenny walked into the bar. There weren't many other options open to her. All the rest was darkness, and passageways without end. She grew tired of wandering, and the bar kept presenting itself to her. She didn't trust its tacky neon façade, with the flashing red sign that said STICKS on and off, on and off. She *knew* it wasn't real. But eventually, when she had passed it four or five times, she summoned up her nerve and went in. Better to die of bad booze, she thought, than of boredom.

Inside it was crowded, but the crowd was indistinct, like an out-of-focus photograph. There was a haze of cigarette smoke over everything. A jukebox blared out some honky redneck tune. She squeezed her way through to the bar.

The barman looked her up and down as the hotel desk clerk had done. 'Sorry,' he said. 'We don't serve minors.'

Jenny opened her mouth to protest. She was nearly twenty, dammit. Then she thought better of it. One or two people in the crowd had turned to stare in her direction already. They seemed to be in fancy dress. She saw a woman dressed in a maid's outfit, and a man in paint-spattered overalls.

Jenny didn't like the way they were looking at her. She didn't like it at all.

'What time's your friend arriving?' one of them asked.

'I don't know what you're talking about,' said Jenny.

'No need to go on the defensive,' said a woman dressed as a nun. 'We're not interested in *you* any more. We know all about *you*. It's your friend we want.'

'Well, you won't get her!' Jenny blurted out. 'She's wise to your game!'

She immediately wished she hadn't spoken. A number of other people were staring at her now. There was a man with a gory stump where his head should have been; the head was tucked under his arm. Jenny thought he looked a little like Barbie's boyfriend, Ken. Through a brief gap in the throng, she thought she could see Paul Lawrence.

He was standing on the far side of the room, drinking beer and braying with laughter at someone's jokes. Jenny thought about going over to talk to him. But then the crowd shifted and she lost sight of him.

One or two people shuffled nearer to Jenny, staring at her curiously. They were all wearing make-up, she realised. It made their faces look unnaturally pale.

'Er, guess I'll be going,' she said, edging backwards.

'You won't get far, little girl,' said a man. His make-up made it look as though his throat had been cut. The loose skin around the wound flapped as he talked. 'All roads lead to Rome down here, you know.'

Jenny backed out of the bar. The man with the cut throat followed her and stood in the doorway. His wound glistened red in the neon light.

'Don't run away, little girl,' he said. 'Things are just hotting up around here.'

'I'm *not* a little girl,' said Jenny. 'Stop calling me that.'

'Oh, but you *are*,' said the man. 'As far as we're concerned, you are.'

'I have to go,' said Jenny. 'Really.' She spun on her heel and headed off down the passageway, trying to look as though she knew where she was going.

* * *

Diana woke up with a start. This time there was no gentle drift towards the surface. One minute she was swimming in the pool, the next she was back in the room.

The green place had been pleasant, not like a nightmare at all. No basement, no fat man, no little girl. She had the drugs to thank for that, she thought. Dreamless sleep, Deborah had said.

But where was she now? The curtain was drawn across the window, but she could see it was dark outside. What day was it? How long had she been asleep?

She sat up. Wires tugged at her flesh. She tore the pieces of sticking plaster off. Somewhere to her left, the small bleeping sound stopped. It was replaced by a low electronic hum.

She wormed free of the blankets and swung her legs over the edge of the bed. The sudden movement made her feel dizzy, but the feeling passed.

She sat there, trying to get her bearings. This was evidently some sort of clinic. Deborah and Oliver had brought her here. If this was where Deborah worked, then fine. She knew how to get home. It wasn't so far away: only a brief taxi ride.

There was a nightlight by the bed. She reached over and switched it on. Her handbag was on the floor. She fished in it hopefully. Her keys were there, but no money. She examined her face in the make-up mirror. She looked tired. Her hair was a mess. She straightened it as best she could.

There was no sign of her clothes, but there was a dirty grey raincoat slung over the back of a chair. She tried it on. It was a man's coat, and much too big, but it covered up her nightgown. Now all she needed were shoes. There was nothing under the bed. She hunted through some of the cupboards that stood along one wall. All she could find amongst the clutter of metal clamps and spare blankets was a pair of pink knitted bedsocks. They were better than nothing. She put them on.

She noticed the small bunch of flowers in a jar by the bed. Freesias. Oliver, she thought. And then she thought no, she mustn't think about Oliver. She would think about him later, but not now. Now there were more important things to be done. She had to find Jenny. Jenny was the only person who could help her understand what was going on. Jenny was the only one who didn't think she was going crazy.

But suppose Jenny had never existed? Diana had never

considered this possibility. She forced herself to consider it now. Suppose Jenny had been a figment of her imagination? Suppose Diana had dreamt her? She shook off the thought. No, she couldn't possibly have invented someone like Jenny. Those clothes, that hair, the way she talked. Diana had never met anyone like that before. Jenny was flesh and blood. Diana was certain of that.

Which made it all the more important that she be found. If Jenny was lost in some sort of limbo, then Diana was the only one who could help. It was up to *her* to find her and bring her back.

She picked up her bag and went out into the corridor.

It was green out there. It reminded her of the place where she had been swimming, but the light was fluorescent: it was too bright and harsh. From somewhere off to her left there came the faint clatter of a typewriter. There was an exit sign at the far end of the passage. She headed towards it.

The doors had small glass panels set into the wood. She looked through some of them as she passed. In one room, she glimpsed an old man, gasping on a bed. He was thin as a skeleton. There were wires attached to his head with small pieces of sticking plaster. He appeared to be tied to the mattress with linen straps. Diana shuddered. She didn't like to think of anyone being tied down like that. She wondered if the old man was part of Deborah's research.

In another room, a plumpish woman was sunk into an armchair. From the blue light on her face and the fixedness of her gaze, Diana guessed she was watching television. The woman's hand rose and fell like an automaton, feeding her mouth with chocolates from a box on her lap.

Diana heard a low murmuring. It was coming from an open door ahead of her. She thought she recognised the sound of Deborah's voice. She crept forward cautiously. She didn't want to get caught and sent back to bed.

Deborah would probably stick another needle in her arm.

She reached the doorway and peeped round it into the room. It took her eyes a few moments to adjust to the flickering darkness.

Then she saw Deborah, sitting next to a man with grey hair. There was a slide projector on a stand beside them. In front of them, projected onto a screen, was a black and white photograph. It was a room. Diana recognised it. She had been there. Charred and twisted shapes littered the floor. One shape, more twisted than the others, lay in the foreground. It was only just recognisable as the husk of what had once been a human being.

'He'd been doused with something,' the man said. 'Probably white spirit, or turps. It's in the report.'

'But it wasn't the cause of death,' said Deborah.

'No,' the man said. 'According to forensic, he was dead before the fire got to him. Probably from loss of blood. His throat had been cut.'

'Horrible,' said Deborah.

The man pressed something in his hand, and the slide changed. The screen was filled by the image of a large, antiquated wardrobe. Something was spilling out of the door: a shape wrapped in sheets that were stained with something dark. An arm dangled uselessly. There was a wedding ring on one finger.

Deborah made a small noise, as though she had suddenly sucked air through her teeth at the sight of the corpse.

'The basement was hardly touched by the fire,' said the man. 'They found the mother there. They reckoned she was dead long before it was started. Maybe by as much as a day.'

'Couldn't he have murdered his wife?' asked Deborah. 'And then killed himself? Or it might have been an intruder. That would be the most logical explanation, surely?'

'Nothing logical about this case,' said the man. 'No sign of forced entry. The suicide theory was the obvious one, of course. But the body was torched *after* death.'

Diana shivered, and not just from the cold that was creeping from the linoleum through the wool of the socks.

There was a brief clattering noise from the slide projector. The image on the screen changed again, and again. Diana saw the hallway and the staircase from her house. She hardly recognised them. The walls were scorched black. Water lay in scummy puddles on the floor.

The next slide clicked into place. Diana gasped. Up there on the screen she saw the face of the little girl, stained with grime and tears. A uniformed policewoman leaned into the side of the frame. Her arm was round the little girl's shoulders. The little girl, evidently, was not comforted by it. Her face stared out of the photograph, lost and frightened.

'There she is,' said the man. 'There's your Jenny.'

Diana clamped her hand over her mouth to stop herself from crying out. It wasn't Jenny. It *couldn't* be Jenny. It wasn't possible.

Deborah appeared to be leaning forward for a closer look. 'I don't know,' she said at length. 'There *could* be a resemblance I suppose. It's difficult to tell. How many years are we talking about? Twelve? Thirteen?'

'Thirteen years to the day,' said the man. 'October the 24th.'

'Maybe the date has a special meaning for her,' said Deborah. 'Maybe she was drawn to the house, subconsciously, on the anniversary of her parents' death.'

'Where is she now?'

'That's just it,' Deborah said. 'She's disappeared.'

For a moment, Diana thought they were talking about *her*. Then she realised. No, they were talking about *Jenny*. She stared at the image on the screen. How *could* this little girl be Jenny?

Yes, she decided, it *was* Jenny.

'She was hiding in the basement,' the man said.

'The basement, yes,' said Deborah.

'We found her in the old wardrobe, with her mother. She was clinging to the body. The trauma must have been severe. It took days before we could get her to open her mouth. But we had to consider the possibility: she might have killed them both. Then put a match to the place.'

'I can't believe it,' said Deborah. '*A six-year-old?*'

'She eventually babbled a lot of nonsense,' said the man. 'About it being Angela's fault. Angela, we gathered, was a figment of her imagination.'

'Ah yes,' said Deborah. 'It's common for children of that age to invent a fantasy friend. Especially when there are no brothers or sisters.'

'And then she prattled on about a lady in grey who had spirited her away from the fire.'

'And there was no lady? Could it have been a neighbour?'

The man was shaking his head. 'They raised the alarm, but none of them actually went into the house. The mother, of course, was already dead, so it couldn't have been her. The child was plainly imagining things. There was no fat man either.'

'Fat man?' queried Deborah. 'I hadn't heard about him.'

The man leafed through a sheaf of papers on his lap. 'According to another of her stories, there was a fat man who had set fire to the house and chased her into the basement.'

'But there were only two bodies,' said Deborah.

'Only two,' the man agreed. 'In the end, it was an open verdict. We couldn't pin it on the kid. And I'll tell you: nobody really wanted to. She'd been through enough. You could tell that just by listening to her. Some of the stories were quite fantastic. To hear her, you'd have thought that the house was a bloody zoo. The place was full of rabbits, she said. The rabbits had gone up in flames. She had rabbits on the brain. She was more upset about the rabbits than she was about her parents. I'll tell you, we combed the house, but there was no sign of a single bloody rabbit.'

'No,' said Deborah. 'The trauma of the experience must have induced hallucinations. Perhaps they even helped her to cope with the reality. Children often do that, you know, make up stories when the reality is too hard for them to bear.'

'And you reckon that this really *is* your Miss Hoffman?'

'I'm almost certain it's the same girl,' said Deborah.

'And she still can't remember anything?'

'She has no idea,' said Deborah. 'It's as though she'd started a whole new life from scratch.'

'Perhaps it would be best if she never found out,' the man suggested. 'It's not a very pleasant skeleton to have popping out of your cupboard.'

'I'm not so sure,' Deborah said. 'It's not entirely healthy, burying such memories for good. They have a tendency to bubble to the surface at inconvenient moments. I think Jenny needs to know, for her own peace of mind. It's best for all of us to confront our fears, rather than suppressing them.'

Diana had heard that one before.

'What about the other girl?' the man asked.

'You mean Diana?'

This time they really were talking about her.

'She's fine. I gave her something to help her relax.'

'You say she's somehow got herself involved in this.'

'Yes,' Deborah said slowly. 'I'm beginning to think Diana is the key to it all. These girls have developed an extraordinary mental bond. They've been sharing hallucinatory experiences, and somehow Jenny's subconscious memories are implanting themselves into Diana's psyche, so that she's reliving Jenny's traumatic experiences in her dreams.'

'In her *dreams*?' The man sounded politely sceptical.

'Yes,' sighed Deborah. 'If only they hadn't cut off our grant, we could be exploring all the possibilities right now. As it is . . .' She sighed again. 'As it is, we're going to have to take more drastic action, or Diana's mind could be permanently damaged. Dr Westmoreland recommends a course of Opthalmoline, but I'm inclined to restore the chemical imbalance with regular doses of Lethadone. Whatever happens, we have to stop her nightmares. She's sinking into a fantasy world.'

Diana didn't like what she was hearing. She didn't like it at all. Perhaps Oliver had been right. Perhaps Deborah was indeed intending to use her as some sort of guinea-pig. Diana felt a rush of anger. Perhaps Deborah really was jealous. Perhaps she'd do anything to stop her marriage to Oliver. The nightmares were horrible, there was no question about that. But, now she thought about it, she didn't relish the prospect of them being taken away from her. They were *her* nightmares, after all. They were part of her. If they took her dreams away, then what would she have left? And how would she be able to help Jenny?

The thought of Jenny spurred her into action. She would have to deal with Deborah later. She slipped away from the doorway and down the green corridor towards the exit sign. Once, she had to duck into the shadow of a cupboard as a man with a clipboard strode purposefully by.

She found herself in the entrance hall. A cleaner, who was waxing the floor, took no notice as she passed.

The double doors gave out onto the night.

Finding a taxi to take her back to the flat was no easy matter. She hailed two which didn't stop. A couple of passers-by stared at her feet. Hey, she thought. *Something wrong with pink bedsocks, then?*

A third cab drew up, then sped off when she confessed she didn't have any money. She was beginning to think she'd have to walk when she spotted a fourth cab. She waved her arms frantically. It pulled up alongside her. This driver looked younger and more sympathetic than the others. Diana told him, simply, that they were trying to keep her in hospital but that she didn't want to stay there. There was money in her flat, she said, and she'd give him a big tip if he drove her back there.

'I got shut up in a hospital once,' the driver said, as they headed towards their destination. 'It was a voluntary commitment. Had some bad habits I wanted to get rid of. But the bastards wanted to keep me there. I got paranoid, I can tell you. They wouldn't believe anything I told them.'

'I know how you must have felt,' said Diana. 'I have that trouble myself, sometimes.'

They pulled up outside Diana's flat.

'You okay?' asked the driver. 'You want me to come in with you?'

'No, I'll be fine,' said Diana, clambering out onto the pavement. 'Thanks anyway, but I'll only be a second. Hold on while I get the money.'

'Forget it,' said the driver, waving her away. 'Glad to be of service. Take care, now. Don't let the bastards grind you down.'

Diana thanked him. She felt more cheerful as she unlocked the door to her flat. At least there were *some* people in the world who didn't think she was absolutely cracked.

*   *   *

I won't give in, thought Jenny. She wouldn't become like those other creeps. They couldn't use her to get to Diana.

She was curled up on the sofa. There was only one

thing worse than stark staring terror, she'd decided, and that was boredom. She was bored now. She had tried looking at books or flicking through magazines, but the back-to-front print had finally got to her. Much better to pretend that the apartment really *was* Diana's apartment, and not merely a replica of it. At least it was more comfortable than the dripping labyrinth outside. At least, here, it was *almost* like everyday life. Okay, so there was nothing outside the windows. But there *was* champagne in the fridge. Jenny had prised the top off the bottle marked enêhcuD-dranaC. The fizzy stuff had gone all over the place, but there was still enough left for a couple more glasses, and it tasted fine. A bubble is a bubble, she decided. Who cared if it was the wrong way round?

She'd drunk some. Now she felt reckless, ready for anything they could throw at her.

She'd blocked out the unsettling blankness of the windows by drawing the curtains across. There might be a whole tribe of little girl zombies out there and she'd never know it. That suited her fine.

The black void, where the mirror should have been over the mantelpiece, was not so easily dealt with. She kept glancing at it nervously. There was a peculiar sense of someone in there, watching. Like the cops on the other side of the two-way mirror when they'd picked her up on that baloney possession charge. She'd got off then. It helped having a father (*foster* father, she corrected herself) who'd done business with some of the fanciest lawyers in Hollywood. He'd given her a bollocking, told her to quit hanging around with street scum. But he'd been there when she needed him.

Well, she needed him now. Only he wasn't here. She was on her own now. Welcome to the Real World. She almost laughed. Real World, *hell*. This was about as *unreal* as you could get.

She got up and went over to the mantelpiece. Tentatively, as she had done many times before, she dipped her fingers into the darkness where the mirror should have been, then snatched them out again. It was like dipping her fingers into ice-cold ink, ink that never stained.

But there was something different about it this time. Was it her imagination, or had she seen a slight movement in there? Had it felt warmer? Was there a lightening of the darkness? Jenny peered closer.

The image developed slowly, like one of the Polaroid photographs she had taken the day before. First of all, she saw the back of the clock, then the wall behind her. The blank space was turning into a mirror. It was beginning to reflect. Jenny reached out and touched. Her fingers came up against hard glass. It was a mirror.

The lounge in the mirror was exactly the same as the one she was in, except that everything was the other way round. Exactly the same, except that she still couldn't see herself reflected in it. In the mirror, where her face should have been, there was tousled blonde hair that looked as though it could have done with a strict brush and comb session. She was staring at the back of someone's head.

Hell, Jenny thought. It was Diana.

She rapped on the glass, 'Diana! I'm here!'

Diana turned round. She looked puzzled, but gave no sign of having seen anything. She was wearing a raincoat that was far too big for her. The collar, turned up around her neck, made her face look smaller and more fragile than ever. Her eyes were ringed with mauve circles that looked almost like bruises. But her mouth was set in a determined line. She looked different, Jenny thought. Not like when they'd first met, at all.

She knocked again, shouting. 'Why can't you see me! I'm *here*!'

Diana didn't react. But she was frowning, thinking

hard. Jenny watched as she backed towards the door, staring into the mirror all the time. Then she pulled the door open and disappeared from view.

Jenny turned round. The door behind her had been closed. Now it was open. Was this a parallel universe, or simply an alternative one? Diana could slip in and out, between the two places. Not necessarily at will, but she could come and go. Somewhere, Jenny reasoned, there had to be a No-Man's-Land where they could meet up. Then Diana would be able to take her back.

She made for the door.

*　*　*

Diana ran down the hallway to the door beneath the stairs. Someone was banging on the other side.

'Jenny?' she called. She heard a muffled shout.

'Jenny!' she called again, tugging at the handle.

For a terrible moment, she thought it was sealed shut. Jenny would never be able to get out. Then the door flew open. The raging snowstorm struck Diana full in the face. She staggered back, rubbing the snow out of her eyes.

Jenny emerged, groping like a blind person, from the blizzard. Diana gave a triumphant yell and hugged her.

'Jenny! Thank God! I thought I'd never find you again!'

'But you did, thank Christ,' said Jenny. She slipped out of Diana's embrace and slammed the door shut on the wind and the snow. 'That's enough special effects for now,' she said. 'Let's get the hell out of here.'

She grabbed hold of Diana's arm and pulled her along the hallway. 'I'm freezing. I never want to see the inside of a basement again as long as I live.'

There was a crash behind them. Diana whirled round. Something was banging on the basement door.

Jenny stared at it, the colour draining out of her face.

'Oh my God!' she gasped. 'They've caught up with us. Quickly! Let me into your flat!'

'My *flat*,' Diana repeated. 'Open the door. It's not locked.'

She looked at Jenny, then at the basement door. She could hear muffled shouting from the other side. Then she looked at Jenny again.

'Show me your fingernails,' she said.

'Diana?' Jenny gaped at her. 'For God's sake! They're *after* us. The fat man's coming!'

'Show me!' Diana insisted. She made a grab for Jenny's arm, but Jenny dodged out of her reach.

'I'm not so sure you *are* Jenny,' Diana said carefully. 'If you're Jenny, then tell me . . . tell me the name of my teddy bear!'

'Don't be ridiculous,' Jenny said. 'You can't expect me to remember that. Come *here*, Diana.' She held out her arms.

Diana backed away, shaking her head. 'You've given yourself away,' she said. 'You should have remembered that. It's some place in Los Angeles, you said. You'd have remembered that if you were *really* Jenny.'

'*Diana* . . .' Jenny's voice took on a threatening tone as she advanced along the hallway. She moved jerkily, like a stiff-limbed puppet.

The thudding from the basement grew more frantic. Diana looked at the door nervously.

'Go ahead, then,' Jenny said. 'Open the door, if that's what you want. See where it gets you.'

There was a soft noise like the splintering of eggshells. Diana stared at her, horrified. Jenny's face was changing. The eyes were sinking into glittering pits. A thin black crack snaked across one of her cheeks. The red mouth stretched into a smile that grew wider and wider.

'Fuck *you*, Diana,' Jenny said in a voice that was far

too deep. 'You think you're *so* smart.' Her fingernails, Diana saw now, were sprouting, growing in front of her eyes into razor-sharp talons.

'You're *not* Jenny!' Diana shouted. 'Get away from me!'

'You're so right, I'm *not* Jenny. I'm *Angela*.

Diana backed into the basement door. She could feel it shuddering as heavy blows rained down on the other side.

In front of her, the thing that had been Jenny stood rocking gently from one foot to the other. There was a noise like milk seeping into breakfast cereal, and the cracked cheek began to bulge.

Diana made up her mind. She decided she'd rather take her chances with whatever was on the other side of the door than face this Jenny mutation. She turned the doorknob. The Jenny-thing opened its mouth and let out an unearthly screech. A black snakelike tongue flicked out through the air and whipped against Diana's neck.

Here goes, thought Diana. She opened the door. A swirl of snow hit her full in the face. Then she felt hands pulling her through the door.

She couldn't see. She heard someone say: 'Diana! Thank God!'

'Jenny! Is it really you?'

'Jeez, I sure hope so. Help me get this door closed.'

They tugged the door shut. The wind howled and tore at their clothes. Jenny's hair was coated with rime. She was shivering violently.

Behind them, in the hallway, the creature screamed with rage.

Diana turned to Jenny. 'Now,' she said. 'Tell me the name of my teddy bear.'

'That's the password, huh?' Jenny screwed up her face in concentration. 'Burbank. No, that's not right. Pico. No, no, it's classier than that. *I* know, it's *Melrose*.'

Diana let out a whoop and kissed her on the cheek. 'It really is you,' she said. 'I was beginning to wonder if I'd ever see you again.'

'That *thing* made it up here ahead of me,' Jenny said. 'It was weird. I could see it changing into me as it came. I hoped you wouldn't fall for it.'

'I'm getting wise to their tricks now,' Diana said. 'Who's Angela?'

'Angela? No idea.'

'You must know,' said Diana. 'Try to remember.'

The creature was still screeching.

'We can't stay here,' said Jenny. 'I'm gonna freeze to death. We'll have to go down again, right? God, am I ever sick of this place.'

'It's the only way,' Diana said.

The wind dropped as they climbed down into the basement. A few snowflakes drifted through the darkness.

Then the storm died. They stood at the bottom of the steps. The passageways led off in all directions. *Business as usual*, Diana thought.

'Which one?' Jenny asked. 'We oughta know our way round by now.'

'It keeps changing,' Diana said. 'That's part of it. The place isn't real.'

'You could've fooled me,' said Jenny. 'You haven't had to spend the night here. It's pretty lousy entertainment. I managed to find a bottle of champagne, though.'

'Let's go ... *this* way,' Diana said. She chose one of the passages at random.

They set off. The darkness immediately swallowed them up. 'Not much fun without a flashlight, is it?' said Jenny's voice.

'Not a lot,' said Diana, wishing she'd remembered to bring the torch with her. 'Hold my hand. Then we won't get separated.'

She felt Jenny's fingers slip into hers and grip them tightly.

'Ugh,' said Jenny's voice.

'What is it?'

'I dunno. I think I just walked into a cobweb. Can't you feel it?'

Diana couldn't. 'Keep going,' she urged.

They plunged on blindly.

Diana thought she could see something up ahead. 'Isn't that a light?' she asked.

There was no answer.

'Jenny?'

Still no answer. Jenny's fingers felt ice-cold.

'Cat got your tongue?' Diana asked, trying to disguise the dread that had crept into her voice. She squeezed Jenny's hand.

There was an answering squeeze. It went on a little too long. Diana felt fingernails digging into her palm. She jerked her hand away.

There was a noise like the squeaking of small wheels. Something brushed by her in the tunnel, and then it was gone. She was alone in the dark.

*　　*　　*

Jenny twisted and turned, trying to free herself from the cobwebs. They clung to her face, wrapping her head in a network of sticky threads. The harder she fought, the more entangled she became.

'Diana!' she shouted. But Diana wasn't there. *Oh shit*, she thought. They'd been separated again.

There was dim light piercing the darkness now. The cobweb wasn't a cobweb after all, she realised. It was a sheet. And she was caught up in it. Where in hell *was* she?

'Come to daddy!' said a familiar voice. It sounded so

familiar now, as though she had been hearing it every day for months. She saw feet. Grey socks and paint-spattered sandals. The feet were coming closer. The feet knew where she was hiding.

In the next instant the dustsheet was whisked up and away. A face bent down close to hers. She saw eyes, distorted by the thick lenses of spectacles.

'You little monster!' the voice growled. A hand shot out and seized her by the wrist. She stared at the fingers. They were smeared with sticky red stuff.

'I know what you did!' the man said. 'You're coming with me, by God!'

'No, I'm not!' Jenny shouted, but she was being dragged out from under the table. She squirmed and dug her heels into the floorboards, but the man didn't seem to feel her weight. He pulled her towards him. Her feet left trails in the dust.

'Leave me alone!' she screamed, beating at his arm. It made no difference. He picked her up. It was as easy as lifting a child. He tucked her under his arm and strode through the door. Jenny felt as though she was being kidnapped by the Jolly Green Giant.

'It wasn't me!' she yelled. 'It was . . . it was *Angela*!'

But who *was* Angela?

'Don't give me that!' he shouted back at her. 'I've had it up to *here* with your bloody stories. But you've gone too far this time. They're going to put you in a place where the *bad* children go. And you'll . . . you'll never get out!'

There was a break in his voice. Jenny saw to her alarm that tears were running down his face. She started to cry as well. She couldn't help it.

They went down some stairs. Jenny banged her head on the bannister, but the man didn't seem to care. She didn't care either. He was angry with her.

She stopped struggling. He carried her across the hall-way and into the studio. She recognised it instantly: the unfinished statues, the figures made from chicken wire half-coated with plaster, the forest glade. The sight of it sent a shock-wave through her. This was it. This was her worst nightmare, the nightmare she had always tried to forget. And she was re-living it.

'Daddy,' she pleaded. 'It wasn't me. It was Angela . . .'

'Shut up,' the man said roughly. 'Shut up and sit down while I phone.'

He pushed Jenny into the glade. She sank down onto a treetrunk and watched as he picked up the phone and dialled a number.

'Daddy . . .' she said.

'Shut up,' he said. He slammed the receiver down, then picked it up and dialled again.

'But daddy,' said Jenny. 'Angela's coming . . . I can hear her. She's coming to get you.'

The man shot her a withering glance. He dialled the number again.

Jenny picked up the nearest rabbit and held it on her lap, stroking its ears. She pretended it was a real rabbit. She thought she saw its nose twitching.

She could hear a scraping, scratching sound in the hallway. A tiny squeaking, scrabbling sound.

Angela was coming down the stairs. She had done something bad to mummy. Now she was coming downstairs. She was going to do something bad to daddy.

'Daddy . . .' Jenny whimpered. She clutched the rabbit.

The man turned his back on her. He didn't want to look at her. He dialled the number again and again.

He had his back to the door.

Angela came in. She was moving with difficulty, because the joints in her legs were stiff.

'Hello, Jenny,' she said in her creaky doll's voice.

'Hello, Angela,' muttered Jenny. She stroked the rabbit. She didn't like Angela any more. She wished Angela would go away.

'We're going to play that game again,' said Angela. 'You know. The one we played before.'

'I don't want to play,' said Jenny.

Angela took no notice of her. 'We didn't finish it last time. The lady came and took you away. But we've been practising ever since. Now you're here, and we can do it properly. This time, we're going to get it right.'

'Daddy . . .' whimpered Jenny. 'Angela's going to get you . . .'

The man tossed his head impatiently. He didn't seem to hear the squeaking, scrabbling sound as Angela moved across the room towards him.

'Ssssh!' she said to Jenny, putting her finger to her mouth. Her fingernails were very long and dirty. 'Don't spoil it.'

She crept up behind the man. Her head came no higher than his knee. She crouched down. She was preparing to leap.

Jenny didn't want to see any more. She closed her eyes.

There was a shout, and a scuffling noise. The shout turned into a scream. Something big and heavy crashed to the floor.

Jenny heard the scream turn into a gurgle. She heard the noise of heels drumming on the floorboards.

The noise stopped.

Jenny opened her eyes. Angela was right in front of her. She looked pleased with herself. Her mouth stretched into a big smile, so big that her face cracked across one cheek.

'Now we change places,' she said.

'No,' said Jenny sullenly. 'I don't want to.'

'The lady's coming,' said Angela. 'She'll get you if we don't change places. You don't want her to get you, do you?'

Jenny said nothing. She stared at Angela's fingernails. They were dripping with something red.

There was a splintering sound. Angela's neck stretched until her head was level with Jenny's. Jenny looked into the cracked, smiling face.

'If you don't change places,' she said. 'I'll get very angry. And you wouldn't like that, would you?'

Jenny shook her head, and looked down at the rabbit.

When she looked up again, Angela had gone. She made herself look round at her father. He was lying on the floor in a pool of red paint. Someone was standing over him: an enormous fat man. His face was all funny: the mouth was in the wrong place. There were long wormy things coming out of it.

The fat man made a squelching, wheezing sound. He twisted the cap off a bottle and turned it upside-down. Liquid glugged out and splashed all over Jenny's father. Some of it splashed on the fat man as well.

The fat man noticed Jenny watching him. 'Helloooo, little girl!' he said. 'Are you ready for the party? Are you ready to swap?'

'No!' said Jenny. 'I won't swap.'

The fat man took a box of matches from his pocket. He struck one and watched it flare up for a moment. He chuckled.

'Here we go!' he said. 'Geronimo!'

He dropped the match.

There was a *whoosh*. The body went up in flames. The fat man stood back quickly, but a tongue of fire had already fastened onto his sleeve. He flapped his arm, squawking, but the flames spread. Oily strips of hair sizzled on his head. He slapped at himself, whirling and shrieking.

Jenny stared. His face was turning to tallow. The fat dripped from his twitching limbs. He lurched towards her, and then the fire roared up and engulfed him. He danced out of the room like a blazing puppet.

She could still hear his screams. They grew fainter and

fainter. Then, quite suddenly, there was a crash. The screaming stopped.

The fire had spread, sending out hungry fingers to eat into the half-formed figures dotted around the room. Carvings flared up and toppled over to feed the blaze. Jenny slumped forward. She could see tongues of flame creeping across the floor towards her. There was a puff of smoke on the edge of the glade, and a stuffed squirrel began to burn. She didn't feel strong enough to get to her feet. She felt detached. She didn't feel as if she were really there. This was happening to someone else. Not her.

There was a shout. She looked up, and saw a grey figure weaving through the smoke towards her. A girl with a wild look on her face.

'Who are you?' Jenny asked.

'Jenny!' the girl said. 'It's me! Diana!'

Jenny tilted her head to one side. She stroked the rabbit.

'For God's sake!' said Diana. She snatched the rabbit and flung it into the flames.

Jenny's face puckered. 'My bunny . . .' she whimpered.

Diana slapped her hard across the face. 'Come *on*! Let's get *out* of here!'

Jenny got up, rubbing her cheek. She let Diana lead her across the burning room. The flames flared up as they passed, then dwindled into darkness behind them.

Jenny leant against the doorway, coughing her lungs out.

'You remember now?' Diana asked.

'I remember,' Jenny gasped. 'Christ, I wish I didn't.' She looked fearfully at Diana. 'It was Angela. She killed them. She was going to kill you too.'

'Who *is* Angela?' Diana asked.

'My doll,' said Jenny. 'No, not my doll. She's the little girl, the basement, everything.'

'She's not the little girl,' said Diana. 'The little girl is you.'

'Not always,' said Jenny. 'Angela sometimes made me swap places with her. I think she wants to swap for *ever*.' She clutched at Diana's arm. 'She's still somewhere around. She's mad at me.'

'Well, we'd better get out, then,' said Diana. 'Are you okay?'

Jenny's eyes were stinging, but she nodded. 'Where are we now?'

'The basement, of course,' Diana said. She looked around, sniffing the air like a hunting dog. 'Over there,' she said. 'Come on. The stairs . . .'

She knew they'd never make it. And she was right. They were within a few feet of the basement steps when the shadows shifted. A shape emerged and blocked their path. It was tall and gaunt, with shoulders hunched like a bird of prey.

'Hello there,' said Paul Lawrence. He rubbed his hands together and his knuckles cracked. 'Going somewhere?'

'Wouldn't *you* like to know,' Diana replied. 'Give our regards to Angela, won't you. Tell her she can go to hell.'

She turned to Jenny. 'Looks like we'll have to resort to Plan B.'

'What the hell's Plan B?' Jenny wanted to know. She followed as Diana started off in the opposite direction, away from the stairway. Paul Lawrence stayed where he was, like a guardian appointed to watch the steps.

'I'm not entirely sure,' Diana confessed. 'But we're bound to think of something.'

'Speak for yourself,' Jenny said.

But Diana did indeed seem to know where she was going. She led the way down the tunnel, barely hesitating when it forked into two. 'It doesn't make much difference which one we choose,' she explained. 'We'll end up in the same place anyway.'

They were in a long corridor lined with doors. Diana tried some of the handles; they were all locked. On each of the doors there was a small printed sign. Jenny read some of them out loud as they passed by: 'Drowning. Falling. Pursuit. Climbing. What *is* this place, Diana?'

Diana shrugged. 'Like I said. Some sort of factory. This is where the dreams get made. Or this is where I *imagine* they get made. It's a strictly limited company.'

'You're telling me,' said Jenny. 'Vampires,' she recited. 'Werewolves. Hey, I reckon they'll have a file on me in there.'

'Nearly there now,' Diana said. 'I can see the end of the line.'

Jenny could see it too. The corridor came to an end. They found themselves looking at the door to the back-to-front flat. It was just as Jenny had left it: ajar.

'Back in Looking-Glass World,' she sighed as they went in. 'I thought I'd seen the last of this place.'

Diana spotted the half-empty bottle of champagne on the coffee table. 'Oh-ho,' she said. 'Emergency rations?'

'Yeah,' Jenny said. 'Look, shouldn't we lock the door? Angela will be coming after us, won't she?'

'Makes no difference,' Diana said, taking a swig straight from the bottle. The champagne wasn't as fizzy as it should have been, but she felt the alcohol recharging her batteries.

'What'll we do now?' asked Jenny, sinking onto the sofa.

'We wait,' Diana said. She sat down beside Jenny and closed her eyes. 'We sit and wait.'

*   *   *

Oliver drove up to the house. There was a light on in the ground-floor window. So Diana *was* here.

Deborah had sounded uneasy when they'd talked on the phone. She had told him that the patient was sleeping soundly. But then she'd slipped up. '. . . when we get her back,' she'd said. *When* we get her back. She'd tried to smooth over her mistake, but it was too late.

He knew, now, that Diana had left the clinic.

He *had* to get to her before Deborah did. If Deborah got to her first, then he could kiss the wedding goodbye. Kiss a lot of other things goodbye, too. Like the good life, his career and the use of his arms and legs. He'd be in traction for months if the boys ever caught up with him.

So Diana was cracking up? Well, that would make it all the easier for him. Just so long as she could recite all the right words when they got to the altar. Then he'd have her declared unfit. She wasn't competent to manage her own affairs. He, Oliver, would be put in charge of them. He'd make sure Diana was okay, make sure she was looked after properly.

And then he'd start converting some of that lovely property into liquid assets. Sell off some of the shares.

The front door was unlocked. Oliver swore. The little fool. She had lost all sense of responsibility. No respect for possessions, no sense of *value*. Well, he'd have to teach her that. He had no intention of sitting back and watching as she frittered her money away. The trouble with Diana was that she was too innocent. She let people take advantage of her.

He saw as he crossed the hallway that she hadn't even bothered to shut the door to the flat. It was standing ajar. *Good God*, thought Oliver. Why didn't she just put a sign outside? *Come on in, everybody. Help yourselves. All you can carry*.

Diana was nowhere to be seen. The flat was just as it had been earlier, when he and Deborah had arrived to take her away. A mess. She hadn't got very far with the unpacking, but what she *had* unpacked was thrown all over the place. The kitchen was full of broken crockery. What the hell had she and that punk American girl been up to? A plate-smashing party?

He frowned, going back into the lounge. The American was a bad influence. She had battened onto Diana like a leech. She'd have to be sent packing as soon as possible. He supposed she would have to be paid off. That was all they ever wanted: money, money, money.

Oliver sighed. It had all been going so smoothly up until this week. Now everything was going wrong. He punched a cushion angrily. He imagined the cushion was Deborah, and punched it again twice as hard.

Calm down, he told himself. He was on edge. The tension was getting to him. He was losing his grip.

He forced himself to relax, and checked his watch. He would give it until midnight. If Diana hadn't materialised by then he'd get the hell out. At least Deborah wasn't likely to be traipsing around at this hour, syringe at the ready. He was tired. He could sort everything out in the morning.

He switched on the television and settled down on the sofa with the remote control, flicking through the channels until he found something with a bit of action. Something with aeroplanes in it.

*   *   *

'Diana?'

Diana had fallen asleep. Jenny tugged at her shoulder. 'Diana! No! Not here! Not now!'

Diana tried to brush Jenny's hand away. 'S'all right,' she muttered. 'I know what I'm doing.'

'Well, I'm glad *one* of us does,' said Jenny. 'Would you mind telling me what you're up to? We're in this together, remember.'

Diana opened her eyes, reluctantly. 'I'm just feeling my way around,' she said. 'Just practising.'

'What do you mean?'

Diana scanned the room, searching for something. 'Look at the clock on the mantelpiece,' she said at last.

She closed her eyes and began to breathe evenly. Asleep again, Jenny thought. This was hopeless. The clock was a clock. There was nothing unusual about it. Except, like everything else in the room, it was back-to-front. The seconds ticked away. Backwards. Time passed, the wrong way, very slowly.

Then, as she watched, the hands on the clockface began to move faster and faster. Soon they were whizzing round so fast she could hardly see them. Seconds and minutes, hours and days.

Diana's eyes snapped open. The hands quivered to a stop. 'See?'

'I don't believe it!' said Jenny. 'That was *you*?'

Diana nodded. 'Now shut up and let me concentrate. Angela's still out there somewhere. I've got to be ready for when she makes her move.'

'What will you do?' asked Jenny, but Diana had closed her eyes again. She seemed to have willed herself deep into some sort of trance.

Were they asleep or awake? Jenny couldn't keep track any more. She thought that maybe she was still trapped in one of Diana's dreams. None of this was really happening; it was all taking place in Diana's head. But, if that was the case, what would happen if Diana started to dream while she was *already* dreaming? The thought tied Jenny's mind in knots. It was like a hall of mirrors: impossible to tell which was reality and which reflection. She gave up, and wandered over to the mantelpiece to examine the clock.

Everything was quiet. It was as if Diana's trick had stopped time itself. The silence was so solid that it almost throbbed. But it *was* throbbing, she realised. It wasn't silence at all. It was a noise like the purring of a giant machine.

It was coming from the mirror.

Jenny listened. It was like the droning of an aeroplane engine, coming nearer, getting louder. Now it was all around her, but she couldn't see anything. It filled her head, vibrating against her eardrums, until she thought she couldn't stand it any longer. Then there was a muffled thump, followed by a shout: 'Fried Jap, going down!'

Jenny peered into the mirror. Neither she nor Diana were anywhere to be seen. But there was a fault in the glass. No, she could make something out. There was someone there, sitting on the sofa where Diana should have been. It was Oliver.

She could see him now, quite clearly. She couldn't think why she hadn't spotted him earlier. He looked dishevelled, unshaven. And tired. His eyes were fixed on something out of the range of her vision. She could hear shooting and explosions. It was the television, Jenny realised. A war film, or something. Of course. There was a set on her side, too, though it was too close to the wall to cast a reflection in the mirror. She thought about switching it on to see what Oliver was watching. Then she thought: no. That business with the radio programme had been bad enough. She wasn't going to risk a repeat broadcast. And, whatever it was, it wasn't interesting enough to hold Oliver's attention. He was trying to stay awake, but his head kept dipping forward.

Jenny went back to the sofa and bent over Diana.

'Diana,' she said. 'Wake up. Oliver's here.'

'Mmm,' Diana murmured drowsily. 'I know.' Her eyes flickered open for an instant, but then she was out of it again. And dreaming, by the look of her; Jenny saw movement beneath her eyelids.

There was a sharp crackle of static. Jenny whirled

round, startled. The back-to-front television had switched itself on.

* * *

The noise jerked Oliver awake. It was too loud. He grabbed the remote control and jabbed the volume button, but it made no difference. The sound was stuck, and something had gone wrong with the picture. The screen was swirling with dark sky and a swarm of tiny winged things. Planes, he thought. No, not planes any more. It looked like a flock of birds. Or bats. Whatever they were, they were flinging themselves towards the camera in a continuous stream.

He must have been dozing. The film had finished while he'd been asleep. It looked as though it had been replaced by one of those pretentious avant-garde videos they sometimes put on late at night. He checked his watch again. It was way past twelve. Time to go. He stood up.

The static stopped, as suddenly as it had begun. Now the silence was broken only by a squeaking, like the noise of tiny wheels which needed oiling. And a faint tapping, a distant skittering, like mice on a sheet of metal. Oliver frowned.

He pressed the 'Off' switch. Nothing happened. He started to swear.

* * *

Jenny bent down in front of the television and gazed into it, almost hypnotised by the dancing fireflies. They swirled and eddied, scattered and regrouped, then flew at the inside of the screen in a five-pronged formation. It was a *hand*, Jenny realised. She jumped back as the fingers struck the screen with a dull crack. The set shuddered and hummed. The hand drew back, and paused, and clenched itself into a fist.

Jenny edged towards the sofa. 'Diana . . .' she whispered. 'I think there's something in the TV. It's trying to get out . . .'

'S'all right,' Diana muttered. 'I know what I'm doing.'

Jenny wasn't so sure. Diana might be a wizard at opening elevator doors and monkeying with clockfaces, but how would that help them when Angela started to strut her stuff in earnest?

The television rocked as the fist pounded at the screen again. The hand retreated into the depths of the picture and unfurled. Jenny saw sharp fingernails springing up like switchblades. It was preparing for another assault. This time, it was going to try and rip its way through.

Jenny was sweating. What was Diana playing at? Why didn't she *do* something? The television screen couldn't keep the hand back for ever. It could force its way through at any minute.

*   *   *

Oliver levelled the remote control and pressed the buttons fiercely, one after the other. The hand dissolved into dancing dots. The squeaking and skittering gave way to a blast of music, followed by a gabble of voices and a distant roaring. The noises ran into one another until there was a cacophony of overlapping soundtrack. It was loud enough to wake the dead.

*   *   *

Jenny covered her ears. The television screen erupted into a riot of images. They flickered and faded as the set jumped from one channel to the next. Jenny saw herself trapped in a dark passageway. She saw Peck falling, and

Paul Lawrence disappearing, and Diana swimming lazily through a mass of deep green water. She saw long-forgotten scenes from her own childhood. She saw Diana, dressed in a long white dress, standing in the doorway of a church. She saw Oliver and Deborah and she saw people she had never seen before in her life. She saw vampires, and red-eyed wolves, and grey-faced corpses clawing their way out of the earth. And then, at last, she saw Angela.

* * *

Oliver pressed the controls again, but the television was no longer responding. He didn't like the doll-face. It was cracked and smiling, like the one Diana had found in the basement. It gave him the creeps, but he couldn't get rid of it. It was on all four channels, and the controls had got stuck; he couldn't turn the damn thing off. It was the last bloody straw, it really was. He felt like throwing something through the screen.

* * *

The face loomed larger and larger. It pressed up against the screen. Jenny saw something squirming in the darkness behind the cracked china. 'Diana!' she whimpered. 'We've got to *do* something!'

Diana was twisting and turning. She began to talk in a slurry voice. 'Wrong . . .' she muttered in her sleep. 'Oliver won't . . . It's *my* dream . . .'

Angela started to laugh. 'That's what *you* think,' she giggled. 'I'll show you what nightmares *really* are!' She laughed and laughed, and then she stopped laughing and butted her head against the screen. The glass bulged outwards under the impact, moulding itself around her face like a thin sheet of latex.

'Little girl!' called Angela. The stretched screen vibrated against her protruding lips. 'Little girl, are you there?'

Jenny felt as if she was trapped in a 3-D movie. The television screen was stretching out towards her. *Comin' At Ya!* she thought numbly. She shrunk back against the mantelpiece, trying to hide.

She had almost forgotten Oliver.

* * *

The television had gone haywire. It was giving off a high-pitched whining which hurt his head. The flashing on the screen was giving him a migraine, and he couldn't turn the bloody thing off. Now it looked as though the whole set was preparing to blow up in his face. Everything was going wrong. Even the *machines* were turning against him. All the lying and the dodging and the pretending of the last few months bubbled up inside him and exploded outwards in a wave of anger. He didn't care if it *was* Diana's television: bloody hell, she could buy another one. He'd had enough. He felt himself snap.

'Jesus Bloody Christ!' he shouted.

He swung his foot at the screen.

There was a noise like a piece of corrugated cardboard being ripped in half. The television disintegrated in a shower of glass and sparks.

* * *

Jenny shielded her face from the blinding flash of white light. Oliver had done something; she didn't know what. There was a buzzing, and a clicking, and then silence. Slowly, hardly daring to look, she uncovered her eyes.

She found herself staring straight into Angela's face.

Angela snarled, and her fingernails came up, slashing and tearing.

Jenny ducked out of the way. She felt something sweep through the air, only inches from her cheek. But the air was empty. She looked around her, dazed and uncomprehending. The television screen was a seething mass of small dots, but it was regular static now: Angela wasn't in there any more. But neither was she in the back-to-front room.

Jenny turned to look into the mirror again. Angela glared back at her. Jenny suddenly understood what had happened. Angela couldn't touch her. She had broken out of the wrong television. She was on the wrong side of the mirror.

Angela squatted on the mantelpiece on the other side of the glass, scrabbling uselessly at the smooth surface. Her teeth had grown long and gnarled. She gnashed them, and a hiss of steam escaped from the corner of her mouth. The long black tongue lashed out. She smashed her head against the glass. She gouged at her face with her fingernails and the last fragments of cracked china fell away.

'I'm coming to get you!' Angela snarled into her reflection through a mouth that belonged to someone else. 'I know you're there! I'm coming down!' She cackled and swivelled away from Jenny and leapt from the mantelpiece onto the floor, leaving a trail of china dust floating like specks of dandruff behind her. She discarded her doll-limbs; they fell to the floor and shattered. She reared herself up to her full height and moved towards the door.

Oliver stepped straight into her path.

Too late, Jenny remembered that he was on the wrong side of the mirror as well. She hammered on the glass. She yelled a warning, but she knew he would never hear it. He was standing frozen to the spot, still clutching the

178

remote control. He looked bemused. Jenny realised that he couldn't see Angela as she really was. He was seeing someone else.

Angela's mouth opened. The voice that came out of it wasn't her own; it was Deborah's. 'Hello, Oliver,' she said. 'I hear your fiancée's been a very naughty girl.'

'Deborah?' he said. 'What *is* this? When did you get here? What the fuck's going on?'

'No!' shouted Jenny. 'It's not Deborah! Don't listen!'

'She's getting ideas above her station,' Angela said in Deborah's voice. 'I think perhaps we ought to put a stop to it, don't you?'

'Is this some sort of trick?' asked Oliver. 'Where's Diana?'

'She's asleep,' said Deborah's voice. 'All we have to do is wake her up, then you can get married and live happily ever after. But we've got to wake her first.'

'No,' said Oliver. 'No, I don't think so. I think we should leave her alone.' There was a strange expression on his face: a quiet determination that Jenny hadn't seen before.

Angela grew impatient. 'We must hurry!' she said. 'She's dreaming about us, you know. You've got to wake her before she dreams us away!'

'You're full of shit,' said Oliver. 'You and this bloody dream business!'

There was fear as well as fury on Angela's face now. 'Get out of my way,' she seethed, edging towards him. 'I'm going down to get her!'

'Oh really?' said Oliver. He folded his arms across his chest. 'Then you'll have to get past me first.'

This was, Jenny knew, the wrong thing to say.

It happened so quickly that she didn't have time to look away. Angela screeched. The long black tongue whipped out of her mouth and wrapped itself like a tentacle around Oliver's neck.

The tentacle tightened its grip. Oliver's eyes lost their focus and began to bulge. The tongue flexed and constricted and began to slice through the layers of flesh and muscle. It latched onto his spinal cord and started to cut into the bone. When the tongue retracted, the head came with it, sailing through the air and hitting the mirror with a sickening thud. It bounced onto the floor and rolled to a halt, the eyes still blinking in surprise. Left headless, the trunk teetered blindly and keeled over like a toppled tree.

There was a red stain on the mirror. It began to trickle down the glass.

Angela turned to smile at the mirror, licking her lips. There was blood on her mouth. Jenny felt faint.

'And now,' Angela said, 'now it's *your* turn, little girl.'

'Oh no, it's not,' Diana muttered in her sleep. 'It's *yours*.'

The dream hadn't gone the way she'd planned it, she hadn't quite got the hang of it yet, but it would have to do. Now it was time to make everything go away. She took a deep breath and dived into the deep green ocean full of bubbles. She floated there, letting her limbs drift, and wiped everything from her mind except the picture of the place where Angela would be going. She saw it in detail: every building, every brick, every speck of dust. She climbed to the top of a crumbling tower and waited. She didn't have to wait long. As soon as she saw Angela approaching, she slipped out of the dream and sealed it up in a small box. Then she dropped the box into the darkest part of the ocean, and swam back up to the surface. Dreams within dreams. It was easy when you knew how.

She opened her eyes.

Jenny was slumped in front of the mantelpiece, staring at the blank space were the mirror had been. There was no reflection. Nothing.

Diana uncurled, stretching like a cat and yawning. 'Have they gone?' she asked.

Jenny looked round at her, bleary-eyed. 'It just vanished,' she said. 'Oliver was there, and Angela . . . They just disappeared.' She reached out to brush her fingers against the ice-cold blackness. 'Did you see what happened? Did you dream it?'

Diana smiled a gracious smile. She might have been at a cocktail party. 'Oliver really put his foot in it,' she said. 'It made Angela come out on the wrong side. She was furious. Instead of getting *us*, she got *him*. Now I've dreamt them both away. It's the best thing all round.'

'You mean you . . . But you can't just dream people away *on purpose*,' Jenny protested. 'Oliver may have been a dickhead, but he didn't deserve to . . .'

'You didn't know him,' Diana snapped. 'He didn't love *me*. He was after my *money*. And I trusted him. I trusted all of them . . .'

Jenny was about to protest again, but something in Diana's face made her think better of it. 'Where did they go?' she asked.

'Look at the television,' said Diana.

Jenny peered into the set, pressing her face against the screen. 'It must be broken,' she said. 'It's still on, but there's no picture. No, wait a minute, I can see something in there.'

The image was fuzzy and shot through with wavy lines. But there was definitely someone there. Angela, or some part of her. She was a long way away. She was almost out of the range of Jenny's vision, but not quite. Something seemed to be keeping her just on the edge of it. She was moving on doll's legs through a dark and misty landscape, over fields of rubble, past crumbling walls. She kept looking over her shoulder.

'It's a ruined city,' Diana explained. 'The buildings

are burnt-out, empty shells. The windows have no glass in them. That's where she'll be living from now on. And she'll be stuck with her doll face. She'll hate that. She won't be able to turn into that *thing* anymore.'

'I can see it,' Jenny said, squinting and trying to focus on the broken buildings. 'There's no one else in the city, right?'

'Wrong,' Diana said. 'Oliver's there.'

'Oliver? I thought he was dead?'

'Oh no. He'll get by. He'll find his head eventually. Then he can either stick it back on his shoulders, or go round with it tucked under his arm. It doesn't make much difference now.'

Diana picked up the champagne bottle and leaned back, satisfied. 'I think I'll send Paul Lawrence there, next time I go to sleep. And Peck, or what's left of him. They can have a party. Angela will probably get mad at them, but all she'll be able to do is hunt them down. She can give them hell, but she won't be able to touch them.'

She tipped her head back and took a mouthful of champagne.

'That oughta be some TV show,' said Jenny. 'Will I be able to watch it, d'you reckon?'

Diana shook her head. 'Only on *this* TV. And we're not going to be here for much longer.'

'But how will you *keep* Angela in the city?' Jenny asked. 'What if she escapes? What if you wake up? What if . . .'

'I'm awake now,' Diana said, smiling. 'Aren't I?'

She drained the champagne bottle and stood up. 'Time for us to return to the real world,' she said. 'Shall we go?'

'I thought you'd never ask,' Jenny said.

They went out of the back-to-front flat. Diana closed the door firmly behind them.

'We won't be going in there again,' she said. The door shimmered and disappeared. They were left standing in the brick-lined passageway. Diana looked around. 'And we won't be coming down here any more.'

The passageway rippled. The floor shivered. They clutched at each other for support. By the time they'd steadied themselves, the basement had reverted to its normal size. The forty-watt bulb cast odd shadows in the brick-lined recesses, but they held no terrors now. Diana patted the boiler as though it were an old friend.

'Hey!' said Jenny, diving into the nearest crate. 'Look what I've found!' She pulled out the china poodle. 'I remember this. This is Fifi.'

Diana was studying the floor intently, as though expecting to find something there. She prowled up and down, then stopped, gazing down almost fearfully, and pounced on a small object that was glittering in the semi-shadow.

'What is it?' asked Jenny.

'My engagement ring,' said Diana, sliding it onto her finger. She looked at it, turning her hand this way and that. Then she sighed, slipped it off and buried it in the pocket of her raincoat.

Jenny slapped her on the back. 'Looks like you got us out of that one, kiddo.' They turned to face each other, hardly daring to believe it was really over. They shook hands, laughing like maniacs, and went upstairs. Up out of the basement.

The door to Diana's flat stood open. They went inside. The living-room was littered with bits of broken glass. There were scorch marks on the carpet and one of the walls. There wasn't much left of the television.

Diana didn't say anything. She fetched a damp cloth from the kitchen and began to clean the mirror.

*   *   *

Everybody agreed that she coped remarkably well.

There was a small item on Page Two of the local newspaper. Jet Hero Jilts Bride-to-Be. Ace Airman Goes AWOL on Eve of Wedding. It was hinted that Oliver Hall had been in some kind of financial trouble. The Fraud Squad announced that they wanted to talk to him. But he seemed to have gone into hiding. His current whereabouts were unknown.

On Page Five of the same edition, there was another item. Two of the *Post and Echo*'s staff had gone missing. The article suggested that their disappearance was not entirely unconnected with a recent well-publicised case of insider dealing. They had either left the country in a hurry, as the writer seemed to think, or they had rubbed up against some unsavoury characters and had been disposed of. This appeared to be an attempt to drum up hot copy where none existed, however. Police were looking into the matter but they, at least, did not suspect foul play.

Diana's father advised her to sell the house, especially when he found out about its history. But she stood firm. She rather liked it there, she said. It would do for now, until she felt like looking around for somewhere else to live. Somehow, she didn't think she'd get round to it for quite some time. It wasn't as if there was any hurry. Not now.

Deborah came to see her once. The meeting was awkward. Deborah asked after her health. Diana informed her crisply that the nightmares had stopped. She said she was glad that Oliver had shown his true colours before it was too late. She said that she would be rather more careful next time in her choice of husbands. Here she shot Deborah a meaningful glance. '*And in my choice of friends*,' she added.

She sent out rather sweet little cards to say that the wedding was off. Nobody was insensitive enough to demand that she return the wedding presents, though Rachel insisted that the full cost of the dress be met. Diana complied graciously.

'Still having those dreams?' Rachel asked, folding the cheque and slipping it into her Filofax.

Diana nodded. 'Yes,' she said. She thought for a bit, and smiled sweetly at Rachel. 'Maybe I'll dream about you one day,' she said.

Jenny spent the next couple of weeks filling in the details of her past. Odd little memories kept coming back to her, like pieces of a jigsaw. She sought out the inspector who had been in charge of the investigation into the fire. She listened as he talked. She saw the slides, and then she listened some more.

'It's funny,' she lied. 'I can remember almost everything, up until the day it happened. Then it's a blank.'

He nodded sympathetically. 'It's probably all for the best. It's not the sort of thing you'd want to remember.'

She agreed. She thought it best not to mention Angela.

Diana had changed. There was a light in her eyes that had never been there before. Sometimes, Jenny felt almost afraid of her. They'd been good friends for a short time, but Diana was already growing away from her. She didn't talk about her dreams any more. Jenny was curious, but she didn't like to ask.

Ten days after Oliver's disappearance, they caught a train from Euston. They took a taxi from the station at the other end. The village was tiny; the High Street consisted of two pubs, and a post office which also sold groceries. There were more churches than shops. One of the churches was St Dunstan's. Diana had dreamt about it often enough, but she wouldn't be getting married there now.

Jenny strolled around the churchyard while Diana had a word with the minister, apologising for all the inconvenience she had caused him. He assured her that there had been no inconvenience at all. She left him in the vestry and came out through the front of the church. She paused by the door. Then, quickly, afraid of changing her mind, she felt in her handbag. The engagement ring made a hollow noise as she dropped it into the collection box. Hollow, but satisfying. Oliver had probably paid an arm and a leg for it.

Jenny was standing in front of one of the graves. 'Hey!' she called to Diana. 'So this is where the Markhams hang out.'

Diana smiled. She looked at the block of granite that marked her grandfather's grave.

Jenny read the inscription out loud. '"Life is a dream: when we sleep we are awake, and when awake we sleep."' She made a wry face. 'I guess your grandpa knew what he was talking about.'

'Oh, he did,' Diana said. 'He did.' She picked up a small bunch of anemones from a neighbouring plot and laid them down on her grandfather's grave. He deserved flowers.

'What will you do now?' she asked Jenny. 'Will you go back to Los Angeles?'

'I guess so,' Jenny said. 'Maybe not right away. I reckon I'll stay here for a few more weeks. Tap into my roots some more.' She looked sideways at Diana. 'I reckon you could do with some company for a while.'

'Yeah,' said Diana. 'I guess so.'

Jenny thought she didn't sound too enthusiastic. Diana liked being on her own these days. She liked to go to bed early, and get up late. Even so, she didn't seem to be getting enough sleep. She dozed off all the time: on trains and in taxis.

Jenny decided that maybe she would go straight back to LA after all.

She craned her neck to look up. 'There's a massive

great cloud up there. Looks like it's going to bucket down with rain at any moment. We'd better get back to the station.'

Diana nodded. They turned and walked towards the gate. The cloud passed over the sun. It got dark very quickly.

*　　*　　*

Diana opened her eyes. Where was she? Where was Jenny? It took her a while to work out what was happening. At first, for an uncomfortable moment, she thought she was back in the clinic.

Then she realised. She was sitting in the fitting room at Kureishi and Co.

'Dozed off there, did you?' asked Rachel.

Diana nodded. 'Yes. Yes, I guess I did.'

Rachel chattered on. Diana took no notice. Her mind was racing. She tried to remember the dream before it faded. This was very important, she knew. Bits of it were drifting out of reach already. She gathered up the remnants in her brain and tried to fit them together.

None of it made sense, of course, but then she didn't expect it to.

This is it, she thought. *The wedding takes place in two weeks time. It's all starting again. And Jenny* . . .

Who *was* Jenny? Diana thought she remembered a face, but she wasn't sure. The memory was fading fast. But how could she expect to remember someone she hadn't yet met?

And Oliver. She was still engaged to Oliver. She was surprised at how disappointed this made her feel.

There was something about a fat man, she decided. And a thin one. And someone called Angela. She hadn't met them either. She didn't really *want* to meet them, but she knew it was inevitable. It was all going to happen, precisely as she'd dreamt it. Well, perhaps not *precisely* . . .

She felt a pinprick on her breast. She looked down, saw the small red bead swell up, just above the neckline of the dress. One of the seamstresses was apologising. Rachel was fussing.

Diana couldn't be bothered with any of it.

It was starting again. She allowed herself a small smile. *Let it start*, she thought. *Let it happen.*

This time, she'd be ready for them. This time, she'd know *exactly* what to do.